P9-CRW-389

THE KING'S CAPTIVE VIRGIN

THE KING'S CAPTIVE VIRGIN

NATALIE ANDERSON

MILLS & BOON

All rights reserved including the right of reproduction in whole or in part in any form. This edition is published by arrangement with Harlequin Books S.A.

This is a work of fiction. Names, characters, places, locations and incidents are purely fictional and bear no relationship to any real life individuals, living or dead, or to any actual places, business establishments, locations, events or incidents. Any resemblance is entirely coincidental.

This book is sold subject to the condition that it shall not, by way of trade or otherwise, be lent, resold, hired out or otherwise circulated without the prior consent of the publisher in any form of binding or cover other than that in which it is published and without a similar condition including this condition being imposed on the subsequent purchaser.

® and TM are trademarks owned and used by the trademark owner and/or its licensee. Trademarks marked with ® are registered with the United Kingdom Patent Office and/or the Office for Harmonisation in the Internal Market and in other countries.

First published in Great Britain 2018
by Mills & Boon, an imprint of HarperCollins*Publishers*
1 London Bridge Street, London, SE1 9GF

Large Print edition 2019

© 2018 Natalie Anderson

ISBN: 978-0-263-07889-3

MIX
Paper from
responsible sources
FSC C007454

This book is produced from independently certified FSC™ paper to ensure responsible forest management. For more information visit www.harpercollins.co.uk/green.

Printed and bound in Great Britain
by CPI Group (UK) Ltd, Croydon, CR0 4YY

For Dave and the kids—here's to a long,
hot, happy summer, playing cards in the
campervan, and thank you for showing
such patience with me for
'just doing another twenty-minute burst'…

CHAPTER ONE

'WHAT DO YOU MEAN, you don't know where she is?' King Giorgos Nicolaides glared at his security chief.

The uniformed man shifted and took two attempts before answering audibly. 'I have the entire team on it now, Your Majesty.'

'Now?' Giorgos, ordinarily so cool that people genuinely believed he had ice in his veins, was lethally close to losing his temper. 'You're telling me that Princess Eleni hasn't been seen since late this morning, yet I am only hearing about it *"now"*?'

It was *hours* after she'd last been seen. It was now evening—dangerously close to darkness.

'She went into the hospital but never made it to the usual ward that she visits.'

Every muscle in Giorgos's body strained as he fought to control his innate instinct to sprint from the palace and start combing the streets for his sister.

Breathe. Think. Assess. 'So where did she go?'

The man before him paled at Giorgos's soft query. 'We're working on that, Your Highness.'

'I assume you've checked all available security footage?'

He fisted his hands in a fierce attempt to hold back the rage threatening to overwhelm him. Why had his supposedly elite security soldiers waited so long before informing him? *Unacceptable.*

'Her guard is to be fired,' he snapped, unable to resist the need to take *some* kind of action. 'As soon as she is found I want him gone.'

'Yes, sir.' The man all but fled from the room.

Giorgos took no satisfaction in knowing that other heads would also roll once the situation was under control, because for now he needed every one of those 'elite' soldiers to be out there trying to find her. Trying to *rescue* her.

Because she'd been taken—Eleni never would have left the hospital willingly. And when he got his hands on the foul bastards who'd stolen her with the intention of doing heaven knew *what*—

He halted his horrendous thoughts and stalked the perimeter of the large room. *Find her.* They just had to find her. *Fast.*

'Sir—'

Giorgos whirled back as the soldier re-entered the room. As he registered the expression in the man's eyes he felt his blood chill. This was a man who'd faced horrors before—not only in war, but in natural disaster rescue and recovery operations. He'd experienced the gamut of human devastation. And right now he looked wary. *Why?*

'What?' he rapped. His brain couldn't compute complete sentences.

'One of the street cameras shows—'

'What?' He stalked forward and gestured at the laptop the man held. 'Show me.'

Impatiently Giorgos stared at the screen. The footage was grainy, but the identity of the woman on the screen was unmistakable. Giorgos watched his younger sister walk alongside a tall man—away from the hospital—to a car parked not far along the quiet side street. He watched as she got into the car and allowed the man to drive her away.

The man who'd held no gun or knife or any kind of discernible weapon. The man who'd almost been smiling. There'd been no apparent coercion, no apparent threat. Giorgos's blood ran so cold he actually shivered.

His sister had *chosen* to leave.

The very night her royal fiancé was flying in to see her she'd run away with another man. And it had taken Giorgos only that one look at the man to know Eleni was in big trouble. That slimeball held his head high and had an arrogance to his long stride. He wasn't afraid to be seen and he clearly knew what he wanted—Princess Eleni Nicolaides. And now it seemed he had her.

The question was why—what was he going to use her *for*? But that answer was also blindingly obvious. The man was a predator, an experienced seducer—Giorgos recognised it instantly because once upon a time he, Giorgos, had been a using bastard like that too.

He clenched his fists, seething with impotent fury. He didn't blame his sister, only himself. She was naive and innocent and young and she'd been duped—no doubt about that. Bitter bile burned the back of his throat. This was entirely his fault. He should have protected her more, should have kept her safer… But heaven knew he'd tried. Right now he couldn't understand *how* this man had got access to her.

'Who is he?' He breathed the question slowly.

Before his security chief could answer Giorgos's mobile rang. He froze, his gaze locked on that of his soldier. They both knew very few people had his personal number. He forced out a breath as he snatched the phone from his pocket and swiped the screen.

'Giorgos, it's me.'

His sister scrambled to speak before he had the chance to.

'Eleni. Where are you?' He was so relieved to hear from her he barked his words like bullets. 'Come back to the palace *now*. Do you have any idea of the trouble you've caused?'

But she didn't answer immediately—and her pause put Giorgos back on high alert.

'I'm not coming back yet, Giorgos. I need time to think.'

'Think? About what?' Giorgos didn't think at all before berating her. 'Your fiancé is already here. Or had you forgotten that you're about to go on tour with him?'

The image of her calmly walking away with that other man replayed in his mind—walking away from her duty, from her country. How could she? He'd never have believed her capable. She'd always embraced her role and been accepting of her future. Everything was perfectly prepared and the plans had been in place for over two years. This was an excellent match for her—she well knew that, as royals, their lives could never entirely be their own.

'I can't do it, Giorgos.'

'Can't do what?' His impatience almost got the better of him.

There was another moment. Giorgos listened closely to the unnatural silence, sensing a new level of danger.

'I'm pregnant,' she said softly.

He closed his eyes, gritting his teeth. He couldn't speak. Couldn't bear to think.

Pregnant.

With one word he was transported back to another time—to another woman. The split-second recollection of the devastation that had ensued slammed into him as if it had been yesterday.

'Prince Xander isn't the father,' she added.

It was his worst nightmare—he'd longed to protect her from exactly this kind of mistake.

'Who?' he finally whispered. *'Who?'* That ferocious anger was unleashed.

'It doesn't matter—'

'I'll kill him. I'll bloody— Tell me his name.'

'No.'

His rage ran unrestrained and he shouted into

the phone. 'Tell me his name, Eleni. I'll have him—'

'Call off the hounds, Giorgos. Or I swear I'll never return. I will disappear.'

His jaw dropped and he was stunned into silence by her interruption. Eleni *never* interrupted him. Never swore or answered back. And she sure as hell never made *threats.* What had happened to his sister?

Again a reprise echoed in his head—of his *own* headstrong argument with his father, his own defiance that had led to such destruction. Recklessness and impulsive action like this led to chaos and calamity. The last thing he wanted was for her to suffer a lifetime of guilt and regret. He knew too well how heavy that burden was.

'It doesn't matter who it was,' she followed up firmly. 'He didn't seduce me. I was a fully willing participant. *I* made the mistake, Giorgos. And I need to fix it. Tell Prince Xander I'm sick. Tell him I ran away. Tell him anything you like. But I'm not marrying him. I'm not coming back. Not yet. Not till I've sorted it out.'

Shock at her rebellion almost made him stagger. 'Are you with him now?'

'I'm not marrying *him* either,' Eleni said.

Giorgos muttered a series of swearwords through gritted teeth. She was so damn naive.

'This child is mine. Pure Nicolaides,' she said. But then her tone softened to include the gentle plea he'd rarely been able to resist. 'And please don't blame Tony for losing track of me. It wasn't his fault.'

'Your protection officer has no idea where you've gone. He's clearly incompetent. He has been dismissed.'

'But it's not his *fault.*' Eleni's voice rose, returning to that uncharacteristic tone of opposition. 'I told him—'

'Lies,' Giorgos snapped. 'But it *is* his fault that he lost track of you. His employment is not your concern.'

'But—'

'You should have thought through the consequences of your actions, Eleni. There are ramifications for *all* the people of Palisades.'

He closed his eyes again. This hurt so much. He needed to make her see sense and stop this foolishness before even more damage was done.

'How do I stop a scandal here, Eleni?' he asked as gently as he was able, making himself focus on her and not his own tortured past.

The past he could not change. But the future? That he *could* help to forge. He would care for his sister however he could. He owed her that, given it was his fault she had no father.

'I'm so sorry,' she said dully. 'I take full responsibility. I'll be in touch when I can.'

Giorgos kept his back to the man in the room long after she'd ended the call, realising how close he was to losing her. That simply was *not* an option. His sister was all that remained of his family and he'd vowed to protect her—and their family name.

'His name is Damon Gale…' his head of security ventured quietly.

Giorgos drew in a deep breath before turning to take on the battle.

'Everything,' he said firmly. 'I need to know every last thing about him. I want all records of him entering and exiting the country. I want to know who he is and what he does—down to what he has for breakfast and what detergent he uses. I want *everything*. Nothing is too small or too trivial to know.'

'We're already putting together a dossier.'

'I want it in less than an hour.' He wanted it *now*.

'Yes, sir.'

Alone once more, Giorgos paced the room as he waited for the vital information to arrive. How had this man got to Eleni? When had he had the chance to seduce her? He'd arranged a perfectly suitable engagement. She would be going from this palace to another nearby. And she'd been pleased—hadn't she? She'd always understood the expectations of her.

He turned as his security chief finally re-entered the room fifteen minutes later.

'We've been running all palace footage through facial recognition software,' he started.

'And?' Giorgos prompted him curtly.

'It seems Mr Gale was a guest at last month's hospital ball.'

'The hospital ball?'

Giorgos was so surprised he dumbly repeated the man's statement. But then he looked at the open laptop the man had carried in. There, frozen on the screen, was proof that this Damon Gale had breached the gates of Giorgos's own damn palace.

A series of four images had been captured from the security footage. The ball—a masquerade—was an annual fundraiser for the hospital, and yet Damon Gale hadn't bothered with a mask even then. He'd walked in with one woman, but had then been caught on camera promenading in the ballroom with another. A tall, slender woman in blue—and even with the mask and the wig she wore Giorgos knew it was his sister.

So the arrogant jerk had seduced Eleni in her own home, under Giorgos's very nose. He'd had the gall to ditch his date while he went princess-hunting.

Giorgos looked back at the first image and could hardly focus for the fury rising through him at the sight of Damon's date. She too wore no mask, and she was stunning. There was pretty and then there was beautiful, and Giorgos had met plenty of both—models, actresses, heiresses—enough to be jaded…spoilt, even. But this was a woman in another league altogether.

Both serene and haughty, while subtly flaunting her sexy curves, her brunette hair was long and thick and hung in a seductive swathe to the narrow waist that was the cinch between her bountiful breasts and curvaceous hips. But even though she had the ultimate hourglass figure, it was her face that was utterly arresting—the pure symmetrical beauty of her wide eyes, upturned nose and pillowy pouting lips.

She was indisputably, classically perfect. Every

inch of her spoke of femininity and sensuality. Her undeniably exquisite features meant she'd be a woman who understood her power and her worth. The dress she'd chosen emphasised that fact—it covered, yet clung, and he knew she'd deliberately chosen it to emphasise every killer curve.

A hot rage brewed deep in Giorgos's belly—he was familiar with beautiful women who toyed with men. Who betrayed them. But *why* had Damon Gale left her side to target Eleni?

'Get me a print-out of this picture,' he snapped.

'Of Mr Gale?'

'Of them both. Who is *she*?'

Why had this man gone to seduce Giorgos's innocent younger sister when he'd walked in with *this* woman? What part did this…this *vixen*…have to play in it?

'Her name is Kassiani Marron. She's known as Kassie and she works at the hospital.'

'*My* hospital?' Giorgos tensed as his fury burned hotter. 'So *she* brought him to the palace?'

'Actually, Mr Gale held the invitation. She accompanied him.'

Giorgos drew in a sharp breath. She was Damon Gale's date—he'd asked her to attend with him yet set his sights on Eleni? Giorgos was stunned. This woman held such sexual allure…

'Ms Marron is Mr Gale's half-sister,' the officer added. 'She is the illegitimate daughter of John Gale, Damon's father, an American diplomat.'

So she was Damon's half-sister—*family*. Of course. It made sense. She was the feminine feline equivalent of her predatory brother. Scalding hot satisfaction rushed through Giorgos's system, flooding his rage and turning into another emotion altogether. An emotion he had no inclination—and no time—to define.

He narrowed his gaze on her image and tried to process the revelation rationally. The vixen would have information. The vixen would have answers. The vixen would *pay*. Adrenalin charged his system like a lightning bolt of electricity, empowering his drive and focus.

He whipped his head up to glare at the security chief. 'Where is she now?'

'At the hospital. Would you like me to bring her to you?'

'No.' Giorgos turned away from the screen with speed. 'I will go to the hospital.'

'Sir?' The officer looked startled.

Giorgos shook his head. As if he could trust *any*

of his security team to deal with this situation, given they'd lost Eleni and not even told him for the better part of the day? No.

No.

This needed urgency, delicacy and above all *control*—the one thing Giorgos had in abundance. He needed to do the interrogation himself. And he'd extract every ounce of information he could from her. By whatever method was necessary.

'Bring my car,' he ordered. 'Immediately.'

'You shouldn't be working late on a Friday night.' The junior doctor leaned over Kassie—too close—with a winning smile. 'You should be coming to dinner with me.'

Kassie took a breath, then answered with well-practised firm but dismissive politeness and eased back from his breach of her personal space. 'I still have half an hour on my shift.'

And she'd be on the ward for at least another hour afterwards. She had too much paperwork to catch up on. Never mind that it was Friday night.

'I have a booking at a very nice restaurant.'

'And of course you don't want that booking going to waste.' Kassie maintained her slight smile, despite the disappointment edging into her.

The guy was probably nice enough, but already her temperature had dropped at the thought. And he was only suggesting dinner—totally tame—anything more intimate would have had her freezing in a nanosecond. Sadly, it was going to be another no from her.

'Fortunately there are plenty of others about to end their shift,' she said.

'But I don't want to go out with any of them. Only you.'

And *there* was a line she'd heard before. 'You don't even know me,' she pointed out gently.

But he'd *heard* about her—she knew that.

'You know Kassie doesn't date anyone in the hospital,' Zoe, one of the nurses, piped up with a smile, quickly shooting Kassie a glance of pure sisterhood solidarity. 'Why don't you ask Terese? She's super-fun and a great dancer.'

Super-fun and a great dancer. Two things Kassie wasn't.

The doctor looked at Kassie, but she avoided his gaze by studying the chart she was carrying, happy to let Zoe rescue her.

He finally turned. 'What about you?' he asked Zoe. 'What are *your* plans tonight?'

Zoe shrugged and her smile turned coquettish. 'You tell me.'

He smiled back. 'Half an hour at the main entrance. I'll be waiting.' He sent Kassie a smug glance and strode down the corridor.

The nurse giggled before he was entirely out of earshot and turned to Kassie. 'Are you sure you didn't want to go out with him, Kassie?' she asked. 'He's totally hot.'

'Dr Hot is all yours.' Kassie sighed deeply. 'And thank you.'

'Oh, no—thank *you*! I'm delighted to take him off your hands.' Reassured, Zoe giggled again. 'I just don't understand why you don't date any of them. If I were you I'd—'

'Be getting back to my work—which is what I'm going to do,' Kassie interrupted swiftly with a firm smile.

But she appreciated Zoe's assistance. It wasn't worth the embarrassment of trying to date any more. She just didn't feel things the way normal people did. But that was fine. She'd long since accepted it and chosen to focus on building her career.

Zoe had turned away and Kassie became conscious of the nurse's sudden silence. In fact the entire ward was abnormally silent. The gentle bubbling hum of soft conversation had ceased. A prickle rasped down her spine and she turned around to see what the issue was.

'Good evening.'

A man stood right in front of her. As she stared up into his face her lips parted but she remained wordless—silenced by the hard glow of his striking green eyes and the furiously cold glare he was directing her way. Dazedly she recognised that this tall, imposing figure wasn't just anyone. She was used to the King's sister, Princess Eleni, visiting the hospital, but not King Giorgos himself.

How long had he been standing there? Had he heard all that conversation? To be caught out talking dating by anyone was mortifying—but by the *King*? Why was he here at all? Why hadn't they been notified? Why hadn't there been the usual security sweep before anyone royal arrived?

A billion thoughts flooded her feeble brain, but the one that her mind locked on to was the most banal and the most unbelievable—*so handsome.* King Giorgos was so incredibly handsome.

She'd lived here all her life but never seen the King up close before—and had certainly never imagined he'd be as good-looking in reality as he was in print. Impossibly, he was more so. As he towered over her she was conscious of his physicality—of the broad shoulders and muscled body that his perfectly tailored suit hinted at. It struck her that the immaculate stitching and fabric was nothing more than a fragile veneer, masking his raw masculinity. His dangerousness.

And where had that *idiot thought come from?*

She mentally slapped herself. So he was tall, dark and handsome? She knew that. Everyone knew that. So what? More importantly, where *was* everyone? Where was her ward manager? She tore her gaze from his to see Zoe a short distance away, walking with a uniformed soldier who must have accompanied the King.

'Don't you know who I am?' he asked.

Her attention snapped back to the column of masculinity blocking her path. Of course she knew who he was.

'Yes, I do,' she muttered breathlessly, instantly mortified by the brevity of her answer. 'Sir,' she added. 'I mean, Your Highness.'

Oh, hell, was she *flustered*? Kassie was *never* flustered.

He was still staring at her. His piercing green gaze narrowed, deepening his frown to appear even more disapproving than before. Another prickle rippled down her spine—and it was not only awareness, it was edged with something *else*. A foreign kind of anger kindled. What was he waiting for? Was he expecting her to curtsey? Bend her knees and scrape the floor? Roll over before him?

But then a sudden image sprang to her mind—of herself on her back and him arching over her—sensual, inappropriate and so unexpected and *shocking* she gasped softly.

His gaze sharpened. 'Will you show me around the ward?' he asked with stinging sarcasm, as if he shouldn't have had to.

The last thing she wanted to do was spend another second in his company when her dormant sensuality had decided to spark up—*and malfunction.*

She cleared her throat, panicking. 'Is there anything in particular you would like to see?'

Why on earth would he want a tour, last thing on a Friday? And, crucially, how quickly could she get this over with so she could step outside and examine the fact that she'd just had a flash of an X-rated fantasy for the first time in her life—*ever*? A totally alien heat flooded her body.

'I'd like to understand what my sister likes to see when she visits.'

Kassie tried to pull on a sympathetic smile and get her mind back on track. 'We missed the Princess today.'

'You usually see her.' He was coldly confirming a fact more than asking a question.

'Every week.' Kassie nodded, happy for the distraction. 'Is she well?'

The icy expression in his eyes instantly slid into steely hostility. She stared back at him, stunned by the animosity so apparent in him. Had the question been rude? Should she not have asked? Why not show concern for the poor woman?

The temperature plummeted as the silence stretched, tearing at her equanimity and customary conciliatory manner.

'The Princess likes to spend time with the younger patients,' she said crisply, deciding to end this as quickly and as politely as possible. Fortunately she was experienced at building barriers to distance herself and end conversations early. 'Most of them are having their dinner and will then be prepared for sleep.'

'Are you saying this is an inconvenient time?'

His query would have been perfectly polite if it hadn't been for that slight edge in his voice.

'It's outside of customary visiting hours,' she replied, with as much diplomacy as she could summon.

'Then let's not disturb them.'

Relief bloomed in Kassie's chest and she managed an actual small smile as she waited for *His Arrogance* to depart. But he too waited, watching her far too closely. His lashes lowered and he lazily looked her up and down. She stiffened. Was he *really* looking at her body? The *King*?

Men had been looking at her body since she was a young teenager and had first developed the curves that so many guys seemed instantly to equate with sexual appetite. They looked, they made assumptions, they made passes. And then they made slurs, because she didn't respond the way they wanted. So, as always, she froze at this visual inspection—but stared hard back at him, glaring to convey her anger at his audacity.

He ended his trailing inspection of her and met her gaze directly, his green eyes imprisoning her attention. She couldn't have torn it away if she'd tried. And, deep within her, an unexpected kernel of energy popped—a spark that set her nerves to smoulder. And then another. Suddenly every muscle tightened, coiling with kinetic energy. Her body *simmered.*

Ordinarily Kassie had no flight-or-fight mode—she simply froze. But now? Now she felt primed to *act.*

He wasn't anything like his serene sister—a sweet woman who liked to laugh and draw pictures for the patients. There was no laughter in him—only leashed energy. She could almost *feel* waves of emotion rolling off him—impatience barely concealed. It didn't seem right for such a big man to stand so still. He was like a predator about to attack. His fiery gaze trained on hers.

She was clearly going crazy. She didn't get flustered in the presence of royals or other supposedly important people. She didn't get overwhelmed. She didn't get struck speechless. And she certainly didn't start thinking about sex. Always she remained cool. More than cool. Outright frosty.

She knew very well that in the doctors' ranks she was famed for her frigidity. That was the only reason why that guy had come to try his luck with her just before. And she'd rejected him—just as she'd rejected every one of the others who'd heard about her and who'd come to ask her on a date. It was no longer about her as a person, but her as a challenge. Rejection from her was a rite of passage for new recruits.

'How else may I help you?' she asked, her throat dry.

'I require your assistance,' he said curtly.

'You need a physiotherapist?'

Insanely, the thought of touching him was…*not what she'd expected.* No, the thought of touching him made the skin beneath her uniform sizzle rather than chill.

Startled by her own stunning inconsistency, Kassie quickly denied him. 'I'm sure there's someone with more experience who can assist—'

'It's you I want,' he snapped.

She flinched. *Want?* What did he mean by 'want'?

She stared up at him, transfixed by the total derailment of her thoughts. By what she thought she could read in the banked heat of his green eyes. Was this some kind of weird pick-up? Because if it was this was worse than any of the attempts she'd been subjected to in the past.

Mortified, she felt as if acid was burning a hole right through her pride.

'Want for what?' She couldn't even speak properly—her voice was reduced to a whisper—but her words were rude.

Because it wasn't quite her pride that was burning—it was something deeper than that. Something more complicated. Had he heard the rumours about her? Was he here to try his luck?

Impossibly, he looked even more remote. 'It is a delicate matter.'

Somehow her brain conflated 'delicate' with *intimate*. Another whisper of a vision—of being close to him—scattered her remaining rationality to the four winds.

Was she *blushing*? She never blushed. Never responded to any suggestion of closeness with anything other than revulsion.

'In what…?' She paused and cleared her throat to force herself to continue, repeating her question. 'In what way do you want me?'

He had not lifted his unyielding stare from her face and she knew he was watching the heated colour mottling her skin. Too late she realised that he *knew*. He saw right thought her and knew the appalling direction her thoughts had taken. And too late she realised the innuendo so blatantly obvious in the question she'd so innocently asked.

'I'm not about to act inappropriately with you,'

he said, very slowly and softly. 'I do have a modicum of self-control.'

He had self-control? Did that mean he *wanted* to act inappropriately with her? She was so shocked she simply couldn't speak.

He took a step closer, his voice lowering further still. 'You need to come to the palace. My assistant will bring you there immediately.'

No. Every instinct warned her against being alone with him. Because even being with him here in public like this was causing a reaction within her that wasn't normal. Not for her.

Emotion surged—fury coalesced with fear and summoned rebellion. She didn't care who he was. She wasn't going to blindly do as she was told.

'I don't get into cars with strangers,' she said as calmly as she could. 'I don't go anywhere without knowing why.'

He regarded her steadily, that arrogant tilt curling his lips. 'Are you defying the express orders of your King?'

She sucked in a breath and replied before thinking clearly. 'Are you abusing your position of power to *control* me?'

His mouth opened and then closed. His nostrils flared as he exhaled. 'Yes,' he said with carefully controlled quietness. 'In this situation I will do whatever it takes to get what I need from you.'

This time *her* jaw dropped. 'I don't see that there's anything I can do—'

'But you don't see everything, do you?' he said sharply. 'You don't *know*.'

'Then tell me.'

'We haven't the time to waste—'

'Then put me in chains,' she snapped. 'That's the only way you'll get me to leave with you.'

Her defiance shocked her. She'd never stood up to anyone so overtly. She worked hard and did as she was told—kept out of trouble and tried to stay invisible to men. But the arrogance of this man was bringing out a side she'd not known she had. Not a good one.

Determinedly she held his stare—and something flickered in his green eyes. She realised he was imagining it—her in chains—and he was enjoying the vision. The heat swamping her now was intolerable, and she dragged in a searing breath as wayward nerves deep within her body fizzed into life.

But suddenly he straightened, and in a blink that cold hostility returned to his expression.

'I need your help with a personal matter,' he

said irritably. 'That is all I am prepared to discuss while we are in a public place. Does that satisfy your safety concerns?'

She was lost for words. How could *she* possibly help him with a personal matter?

His gaze narrowed. 'Have I given you reason not to trust me?'

'I don't trust anyone,' she answered honestly.

Not intimately. And she certainly didn't trust *him*. King Giorgos had a good reputation—he was serious, intense, and it was known that he worked hard and long hours—but that edginess he carried, and the unexpected, unexplained demand he was making…

Her body was sending out all kinds of chaos signals—the shivers down her spine, the speed of her pulse, the breathlessness, the *heat*. Maybe she was coming down with something. But, no, in her gut she didn't trust anyone—not him, and now she was beginning not to trust herself.

His smile was slow and not very reassuring. 'No doubt you have your reasons.'

Of course she did. 'Several,' she replied coldly.

He offered nothing more than a dismissive shrug. 'Regardless of your hesitation, we need to leave.'

She shook her head. 'I have to finish my shift.'

'Leaving a few minutes early will make little difference. Your manager has already been informed.'

Shocked, she stared up at him, registering his planning. He hadn't come to the hospital to visit patients and to spread cheer.

'I came here for you.' He quietly confirmed her thinking. 'And I'm not leaving without you. If I have to get my security team to forcibly remove you, then that's what I will do.'

'No, you won't,' she challenged him—because this she *did* know. 'You care too much about what people think.'

King Giorgos was remote and dignified and there'd never been a breath of scandal about him. He was *Giorgos the Perfect*, while his sister was *Eleni the Pure*.

He blinked rapidly. 'I beg your pardon?'

'You're the hard-working, serious King who can do no wrong.'

'You *do* realise you're insulting that "hard-working, serious King" to his face?'

'Because he *is* doing wrong. You can't *make* me go with you.'

'I can—because this is too important. We are leaving,' he ordered. 'Walk with me now.'

'You're serious?'

He took another step closer—a shade too far into her personal space. 'Are you going to make me get the chains? Because if that's really what you want, then of course I wouldn't dream of disappointing a lady.'

His sneer was mortifying. That humiliating blush burned again. She hadn't meant it about the chains, yet here he was implying that she was doing this only to…to *flirt*? She *never* flirted.

What was wrong with her? This man made all the rules—he owned the nation…his face was on the currency—and she was snapping at him like some schoolgirl with an immature crush.

'Of course not.' She avoided his eyes and muttered contritely, 'I'll just get my bag and then we can leave.'

She was startled when he kept pace with her as she went into the small office.

'Why are you following me?'

'I'm not giving you a chance to hide anything or any time alone to contact him.'

Contact who? She stared at him uncomprehendingly.

'Just get your things,' he muttered.

It finally dawned on her that this had to be a case of mistaken identity—he'd confused her with someone else and there was nothing *she* could help him with. *She* was nobody. She did nothing but work at the hospital and then go home to read up about more work. But she'd go with his assistant now and they'd soon realise she wasn't the person the King sought. Then they'd bring her back here and all would be forgotten.

Reassured by this reasoning, Kassie grabbed her satchel and slung the strap over her shoulder.

She almost had to run to keep pace with him moving through the hospital. He'd lost patience and wasn't slow. She stepped into the sleek black car idling right outside the back entrance. To her surprise King Giorgos walked around and got into the seat on the other side.

'I thought I was going with your assistant?' she said. She'd been looking forward to a quick resolution.

He directed a quelling look at her as the car glided off, taking them away. 'Do you *ever* stop questioning?'

'Not when there's this much to be questioned. Where are you taking me? And why?'

'*I'm* the one who has the questions, Ms Marron.'

The edge in his tone forced her to regard him directly. Something lurked in the back of his eyes—a streak of wildness that surprised her.

But it wasn't entirely a surprise. From what she'd seen of him at a distance—in the news and on the television—King Giorgos had always appeared to her like a wild man forced into refined clothes. It wasn't that he wasn't civilised—of course he was—but it was as if he might break free from the polished uniform at any moment. He was too elemental to be contained.

Idiot.

She scoffed at her wayward thinking. She was just unused to a man his size. He was taller than average, with a powerful set to his extremely broad shoulders. Lean and muscled, his physique and demeanour were imposing. And this close she could see his hair was a little bit too long, and a faint edge of stubble showed on his jaw, adding to the impression of edginess—of a man chafing at his constraints. And right now he was clearly inwardly struggling to contain a fierce emotion.

But the thought that King Giorgos might be struggling with latent rebelliousness was pure imagination. This was *King Giorgos*. The man had been King since his late teens—earnest and capable beyond his years. Yet suddenly all she could do was think about that streak of wildness and the size of his muscular thighs and the promise of physical power…

What was *wrong* with her? She swallowed, but it didn't ease the dryness in her throat.

She realised that he was silently scrutinising her as much as she was him. But he had that hostility in his eyes again, and a moody set to his jaw. His whole positioning was tense. Something was off. Something was wrong. And she had no idea how she was supposed to help.

'Is it Princess Eleni?' she asked softly.

He sat very still. 'What makes you say that?'

'She missed her visit today. She never misses her visits.'

He watched her…waiting. Something swirled in the atmosphere between them. The luxurious car suddenly felt cramped—as if she were too close to him, as if he could see into her mind. She felt compelled to fill the silence—anything to deflect this pull she felt, pushing her nearer to him.

'She was unwell last week,' she added, licking her dry lips.

'Unwell in what way?'

Foreboding slithered down her spine at the ice in his voice.

'She was dizzy. She said she'd had a bug recently.' She frowned as she swallowed again. 'Is she okay?'

If she wasn't then the King ought to be summoning a doctor, not a physiotherapist.

'Did anyone else notice that she was unwell?' he asked. 'Did anyone ask about her?'

Kassie shook her head—then froze. Damon, her half-brother, had appeared just after the Princess had walked away. He'd asked her who she'd been talking to. Now she thought about it, Damon had been *too* curious—and stunned when he'd learned the Princess's identity. Why had he been so surprised?

'Ms Marron?' the King prompted.

Chills whipped across her skin, chafing where heat had burned only moments ago. Perhaps this *wasn't* a case of mistaken identity. Perhaps there was something *very* wrong. She barely knew her half-brother, Damon, but she wasn't about to throw him under a bus. Not until she understood exactly what was going on.

King Giorgos's expression hardened as she remained silent. He knew she was holding something back. How did he *know* that?

'You attended a ball at the palace a few weeks ago,' he said coldly.

'Yes.' There was no point in lying—but she didn't need to offer any more information than necessary, right?

'Why?'

Her heart thumped. 'It was for charity. For the hospital.'

'But you didn't go with the hospital staff. You attended as the guest of someone else.'

She hadn't been one of the lucky staff to win a lottery invitation, but Damon had taken her—the only thing she'd let herself take from the half-brother she'd met only a few months before. Damon had seemed preoccupied when they'd left the ball, but she'd been too deep in thought herself to notice much; she didn't really know him well enough to ask if he was okay. She should have asked.

But then Damon had asked that random question—more than once. *'Did you see that woman in the blue wig and black mask? Do you know who she is?'*

Kassie hadn't even seen who he'd meant—

there'd been plenty of women in wigs…it had been a masquerade ball, after all. It could have been anyone, right? But not Princess Eleni. Everyone knew that the Princess hadn't attended the ball that night because she'd been unwell with a migraine.

But once more Kassie remembered the look of utter astonishment on Damon's face when he'd learned that Princess Eleni was the visitor he'd overheard at the hospital that day a few weeks later.

'You see my sister every week. I hear she likes to talk to you?'

She hadn't answered King Giorgos's earlier question. She realised now he hadn't needed her to because he already knew. Just as he already knew the answer to this question too.

'I take her on her tour of the ward, yes.'

'And when she was unwell last week…?'

'She didn't stay. No one else was aware she was unwell.' None of the other staff, nor the other patients.

'No one?' he pressed, astute and seeking. 'What aren't you telling me?'

She panicked, desperate to deflect his questioning. 'Your sister might put up with your bullying, but I'm not going to.'

He stiffened. 'That's what she told you? That I bully her?'

She couldn't hold his scorching gaze, and was unable to lie. 'No. I never spoke with her about anything personal. She never mentioned you.'

Her foolish eyes had minds of their own and they couldn't resist looking into his again. He kept watching her, and suddenly nothing else seemed to register or matter. Nothing but this moment in which the world tilted, shifting something within her. Something deep and profound and *frightening*.

She forced herself to glance away, but he reached out and touched her chin, drawing her gaze back to his. There was no veil over his expression now. He was lethally, icily angry.

'Tell me everything you know,' he ordered.

'Or what?' That deep curl of fear forced the defiance from her—a primitive instinct to hold him at bay even though she knew it was rude, perhaps wrong. 'You're going to torture me?'

'It's a tempting thought,' he muttered. 'And you seem to like the idea of chains. But I can think of a *better* way to extract the information I need.' His eyes narrowed. 'A more fitting way.'

She couldn't breathe. His words—his promise—sucked all the air from her lungs.

The opening of the car door startled her. Only then did she realise that they were inside the palace grounds. The large iron gates had automatically closed behind them. Locking her in.

'Come into my palace,' he demanded, curtly exiting the car to stalk ahead of her.

'Said the spider to the fly…' she muttered beneath her breath in annoyance at his peremptory tone and total lack of manners.

He stopped walking and spun so quickly she almost bumped into him from behind. *Damn*, it seemed the man had supersonic hearing.

'You think I'm going to make you my prisoner?' he asked, so softly that all illusions of her personal safety were shattered.

King Giorgos was pure predator and she'd never felt in so much danger. Nor had she ever felt such primitive exhilaration.

Suddenly she wanted to sprint from him. Instead, as always, she froze.

'You think I'm going to eat you?' he added with the slightest huskiness.

It wasn't the sexual innuendo that shocked her but her sudden sensual response to it. Another of those incredible flushes burned her at the blatant carnality of his taunt.

'I think I'm right to be wary.' She pushed the words past the croak in her throat.

'Because you're guilty as sin?'

Kassie squared her shoulders and made herself look directly into his shadowed, judging eyes. 'What exactly is it you think I'm guilty of?'

CHAPTER TWO

RIGHT NOW GIORGOS could believe her guilty of nothing. And everything.

Kassiani Marron wasn't what he'd expected—she was much, much more. More beautiful than the pictures from the ball—impossible as he'd thought that could be, especially considering she was wearing the most horrendous uniform he'd had the misfortune to clap his eyes on. And in his decade as King he'd seen a million uniforms.

This was a drab, shapeless tunic with a high collar that revealed no skin whatsoever, paired with black trousers and utilitarian shoes. Her stunning hair was swept back into a neat braid and she'd not applied any make-up to accentuate those thick curling eyelashes framing her enchanting deep brown eyes. Nor had she bothered to rub any gloss on her full, kissable pout.

Because she didn't need to.

Because despite this apparent lack of artifice, and despite the dullness of her attire, she'd easily capture the attention of any red-blooded man in her vicinity.

Frustration bit hard, forcing him to grit his teeth. He was hardly about to demand that she strip. Because wasn't that what she wanted? Wasn't she playing her part in a honey trap? Wasn't the sexual undertone to every word spoken between them part of her plan?

He'd watched her shoot down that doctor who'd asked her on a date with the coolness of an ice queen. The poor guy had been so transfixed by her he hadn't even noticed his King standing at a little distance just behind her. He could understand the man's focus. She made it impossible to pay attention to anything else when she was in the room, with the dazed sensuality of her wide-eyed gaze and parted-lips pout. It was a wonder there hadn't been any medical malpractice cases at the hospital.

So he'd keep the lights on low and not let himself be blinded by her exquisite features. He needed information from her—that was all. He refused to be taken in by her manipulative flirtation or her challenges.

He led her down the darkened corridors, not taking her to the formal meeting room as he'd planned. He needed more privacy than that, and he needed the control he felt in his personal quarters. He had years of self-imposed restraint behind him—this meeting with her would be entirely manageable.

'Are you taking me to the dungeons?'

And there it was—another sultry challenge to his control. Her breathy voice prodded his simmering anger. She had no reason to defy him if she wasn't guilty. Her attempt wasn't going to work the way she wanted it to.

'As I have already said,' he answered softly, 'I'll use whatever methods are required to extract all information.'

He felt her slight misstep, as if she were shocked. As if she were afraid he really *was* going to take her to a torture chamber. Another ripple of awareness swept over him and he gritted his teeth harder. Oh, she was so very skilled, with those sensual words and those eyes, while somehow sending a blush of innocence and naivety sweeping over every inch of her luminous skin.

He stepped aside for her to enter his suite ahead of him. He watched her glance about the dimly lit room, her mouth held firm, her shoulders tense as she looked everywhere but at him.

Irritated that he ached for her attention, he snapped his first question. 'You went with Damon Gale to the ball. Why?'

She turned to stare at him briefly.

'Just answer,' he growled. He had no patience left for her games.

She glanced at the dark-toned painting hanging on the wall rather than addressing him directly. 'He introduced me to a couple of medical technology investors and a robotics researcher.'

Giorgos frowned. So it had been a business meeting? He didn't think so. 'And to return the favour that night you introduced him to Eleni?'

Wariness bloomed in her eyes. 'Princess Eleni wasn't there.'

'She was—and you introduced them.'

Kassiani shook her head. 'She wasn't there. I didn't see her.' She puffed out a breath. 'I heard that she was unwell—that's why she wasn't at the ball. And I never would have presumed to speak with her even if she had been. She's the *Princess*.'

Giorgos paused. Veracity rang clear in her voice like the echo of a pure bell.

Disconcerted, he chose another angle. 'But you told Damon when he could find Eleni at the hospital?'

Damon had returned to Palisades for a number of short visits since the ball. And he'd been to the hospital each time. She flushed and her gaze dropped. She couldn't deny that.

Rage gripped him and he tensed, holding himself back from shaking her. 'You told him. And then he took her.'

Her jaw dropped and she lifted her long lashes, turning a stunned look upon him. '*Took* her?'

'Where?' He stepped closer, no longer caring about protocol and personal space and not buying into her plan. 'Where did he take her?'

'Eleni's *missing*?'

'Don't act as if you don't know.' He grabbed her upper arms, unable to hold back a second longer. He needed her to realise how serious this was.

Needed to feel her skin.

It was soft and silky and instantly he wanted to touch more.

'What was the plan?' he asked harshly, restraining his wayward thoughts. 'We know they've gone on his boat. Where is it going? Where is he taking her?'

'What do you mean, they've gone on his boat?' Kassiani's soulful eyes were wide and her kissable lips parted in surprise.

'Are you saying Eleni isn't here?'

'Tell me everything,' he growled, somehow pulling her closer still.

'I don't *know* anything.'

Frustration bubbled over. How did she dare to be so heartbreakingly beautiful as she looked up at him with those passionate eyes and lied to him? How could she have the face of an angel but the soul of a liar and a cheat? How could she manipulate her sensuality to ensnare her victims?

'Sleep with lots of the surgeons, do you?' he snarled at her.

She flinched, but kept her gaze trained on him. He stilled, watching anger supersede that other undefined emotion in her molten brown eyes.

'You have no right to question me about my personal life,' she said with cool dignity. 'That's harassment. Whatever your problem is, it has nothing to do with me.'

'*Doesn't* it?' He had the feeling it had everything to do with her.

But she was right. He shouldn't have asked her that. He wanted to cut out his tongue for that stupid lapse in control. Wasn't it exactly what she'd been pushing him to with her mention of chains and dungeons and torture? Wasn't this underlying sexual element to their conversation exactly what she'd planned?

He'd fallen into her trap.

He released her instantly. He shouldn't have crossed that boundary. He always kept his distance and discretion, never mixing women into his public life. At least not since he'd been crowned and had determined to prove himself to those disapproving courtiers who'd blamed him—rightly—for his father's premature death.

But he'd been off balance from the moment he'd seen her image on that screen. He was thunderingly furious—how could he have got so distracted? His sister was alone out there—*pregnant*—and yet he couldn't concentrate on finding her because all he could think about was how stunning this woman was. All he felt was this appalling urge to touch Kassiani more. To wreak his revenge—and bury his guilt—in the most pleasurable of ways. To have her surrender everything to him—her information and then her body.

He jerked back, releasing her to reassert his teetering self-control. Clearly it had been too long since his last affair.

'Tell me about the night of the ball.'

Her tongue touched her pillowy lips. Giorgos

turned completely away, unable to bear looking at her a second longer. He ran his hand through his hair as a hot wave of anger engulfed him. Determined to dispel the claustrophobic feeling, he jerkily stripped out of his suit jacket and wrenched off his tie. He saw her gaze follow the ribbon of silk as he threw it across the room to a low chair.

'I barely know Damon. There's nothing I can tell you,' she answered, still watching as he unclasped his cufflinks and rolled his stiff shirt-sleeves to three-quarters. Her eyes widened as he worked and her skin pinkened again.

'Eleni was in disguise at that ball.' He ground out the shocking fact he'd discovered. 'Deliberately. She went to meet him and *you* helped them.'

'No.' She shook her head. 'Damon only decided to go at the last minute, when he realised that it would help me. Because he could get me those introductions. He hadn't planned to meet with the Princess. There's no conspiracy there.'

'Wrong,' Giorgos argued obstinately. 'He planned this. He's taken advantage of her.'

'Perhaps she took advantage of *him*?'

Never. 'She's alone out there with that philandering jerk while her fiancé is *here*, waiting for her.'

'The fiancé *you* selected for her,' Kassiani

needled. 'And perhaps Eleni seduced Damon? Mightn't that be possible?'

Because that was what *she* would do? She was a vixen—so certain of her sensual power. But Eleni had been raised in a world with vastly different expectations and duties.

'*You* might be a mistress of seduction, but my sister is not the kind of woman you are.'

She actually coloured more, and he heard another hitch in her breath. Why did he have such a visceral sexual response to this woman? Especially when he was certain she was toying with him.

Angrily he strode across the room to switch the lights on full, needing to shatter the thickened atmosphere with its sense of intimacy.

She blinked and then looked about the room again with undisguised disapproval. 'This is one of your meeting chambers?'

'Actually, this is part of my private suite.'

She turned those stunningly soulful eyes on him, they were now widened with something akin to horror. 'You *choose* to live like this?'

Like what? He rested his hands on his hips and stared at her, daring her to voice her sultry criticism.

'It's like a mausoleum in here.' She waved a

graceful hand in the air. 'Impersonal dry paintings, uncomfortable antique furniture...' She turned a sharp gaze on him. 'And a cold, controlled atmosphere.'

She was trying to bait him, but it wasn't going to work. 'This palace has been impeccably maintained,' he said shortly.

'I can see that. There's not a speck of dust. Not a painting out of place. The whole palace *appears* perfect. Just like you.'

'What does that mean?'

'It's all a gilt facade—there is nothing beneath. No story. No soul.'

'After five minutes alone with your King you have come to such a flattering snap judgement?' He growled caustically. 'What makes you so certain I'm cold?'

Who did she think she was to insult him? Her daring smacked of manipulation once again. And the worst thing was that it was working. Sensual heat had turned his bones to cinders. All he wanted was to slam her against him so he could assuage the ache of his hard body against her lush softness. God, he wanted her surrender. For the first time in a decade he didn't have complete control of a situation and he wanted to claim *some* part of it back.

'Your plans for your sister…' she said, too calmly. 'You're not really worried about her—you're worried about how this all looks.'

He stilled. He didn't care about her insulting his decor, but she didn't get to opine on his relationship with Eleni. She didn't get to question his loyalty. 'I'm *not* worried about my sister?'

'Clearly not,' she said, dropping the mocking smile. 'When you're insisting on marrying her off. You're using her for royal publicity. This is all about the Nicolaides machine.'

'This marriage is for her protection,' he said coldly.

The scepticism in her eyes was like an acid peel on his heart. 'Protection from *what*?' She glanced about the room again. 'When she lives in a prison like this?'

She made it sound as if it were horrible. 'You have no idea of the pressure she faces. The relentless public scrutiny. They circle her like sharks.'

The pressures on Eleni were untenable. It was bad enough for *him* to have to bear, but worse for the women of the family. The judgement was intolerable. The expectations too high.

'So your answer is to send her from one prison to another?'

'Royals marry royals,' he said icily. 'It is best that way.' Only those reared within the system had the tolerance and the acceptance.

'But not you,' she pointed out. 'You're almost a decade older than she is, yet you're still not married. What about *your* well-being and protection?'

Oh, he was well aware of his duty, and he had a plan for when the time was right. But he felt Eleni needed security sooner. And he was right.

'Is it so wrong to want my sister to be happy and well cared for?'

He was incensed by her judgement. She knew nothing of what life in this palace was like. She knew nothing about his sister. Eleni was an innocent, naive young woman who'd been sheltered her entire life while at the same time juggling immense pressure. Whereas the woman before him now was more than worldly, more than aware of her sensual power. She knew exactly how to wield it. She'd brought a whole hospital full of doctors to their knees—and the horrendous uniform only served to expedite their stripping fantasies.

'By marrying a playboy jerk who was never going to be faithful to her?'

Yeah, she knew *nothing*. 'You shouldn't read the tabloids,' he mocked, unconsciously stepping closer. 'Nothing of what they print is true.'

'So nothing of what they say about you is true either?' she fired back, stepping up to face him square-on. 'You're *not* honourable or kind or devoted to your duty?' She laughed bitterly. 'Are you saying that behind your perfect reputation there's a monster?'

'I don't mind being a monster if by that you mean I'm doing the right thing. Your brother has stolen the most precious thing in my life. He has hurt her. He will pay.' He was beyond angry—he was hurt.

'The most precious *"thing"*? That's what she is to you? A commodity to be bartered? A possession?'

'It is a figure of speech,' he snapped. 'Nothing and no one is more important to me than Eleni. She is my responsibility. She is—' He broke off.

He didn't want to admit such personal truths to this shallow Siren. Didn't want to confess that he didn't want Eleni to make a mistake that could have the same consequences.

He glowered at Kassiani, somehow right in front of her now, as he tried to stay in control. 'You do not get to judge my family. You do not get to judge *me*.'

'I do when you're punishing me for something you think my half-brother has done. Something I don't even know. Where's the fairness in that?'

Her anger was unwarranted. 'In what way am I "punishing" you?'

'By bringing me here against my will.'

'Just give me the information I need. It's simple.'

'There's nothing I can tell you. I barely know him.'

'There's plenty you can tell me. You're choosing not to.'

Her jaw dropped. 'No wonder Eleni ran away from here. From *you*.'

He braced himself against the flinch her words caused. 'Because…?'

'Because of your inability to *listen*. You say I don't get to judge? But that's *all* you do. You don't need me here—you've already worked out everything on your own and you only want me to confirm your theories. You're not actually willing to consider an alternative, let alone the *truth*. I bet you haven't even considered Eleni's own wishes. Do you even know what they are?'

Her accusations had hit a nerve. Rage and regret clouded his reason, making the last of his self-control splinter.

'When did you last talk to her about her marriage?' Kassiani pressed, clearly aware that she'd struck a raw spot. 'Did you talk to her at *all*?'

'Be quiet!' he snapped, reaching out to grab her hips and *make* her listen. 'You say I'm not willing to consider an alternative?' he jeered. 'What alternative are *you* suggesting—with your delays, your attempts not just to distract but to provoke me? Is *this* what you want me to do? Retaliate?'

He hauled her that last inch closer, until she was pressed against him. Until there was no denying the reaction he had to her.

'Fine,' he snarled. 'Win what you want. But I want to know *why*?'

Kassie couldn't speak. She had no idea why. This could have been settled so simply in a five-minute quiet conversation, but the second he'd appeared before her she'd reacted to him with such intensity.

The need to push back against his arrogant orders had been visceral. She'd operated not on thought, but on instinct. And the terrible thing was that her instincts were telling her to push in another way now. To push closer still. It was terrifying, but her physical awareness of him was so acute it almost hurt. His thighs were pressed against hers, and his rock-hard abs and his masculine arousal were evident between them.

Shocking. But it was more than that. It was thrilling.

His green eyes gleamed as he towered over her. Having shed the jacket and tie he looked less civilised—more like the man she'd somehow known him to be. With that wildness uncaged, with the constraints of polite society vanished, he was all ferocity. All power. She'd suspected that he was *built*, but this was ridiculous.

A feeling deep inside her began to unfurl—one that had been so tightly bound that its snaking, unfettered release was too good. *Irresistible.* Her pulse pounded loud in her ears as her blood raced like quicksilver.

'Is this what you want?' His voice was hoarse as he asked again, his muscles straining.

'No…' But her voice was so constricted only a whisper emerged.

She'd never wanted a man close like this. Holding her. Caressing her whole body with just a breath. And yet deep within there was a softening, even as another tension coiled tightly. For once she wasn't cold—not frigid with distaste and stiffly rejecting the contact. No, right now she was burning with a fever such as she'd never known. And the only way to ease it even slightly was to rub against the press of his body. He was both the source and the cure for this contagion. His arms were tight bands about her—the welcome bars of a prison she'd never have believed she'd ever wish for.

His hand cupped the side of her face, holding her so she couldn't turn her gaze from his. Powerful, searching, his eyes held not just hostility now, but arousal too. Anger laced with lust. She was transfixed, but not frozen. She'd gone from feeling nothing to feeling everything. To yearning for something she'd never before wanted or even understood.

'Me neither,' he gritted. 'I don't want to stand here. I don't want to hold you. I don't want to want you.'

And all the while his gaze saw right through her. All the while his head lowered, bringing his mouth nearer to hers.

'You're a liar,' she whispered shakily.

'So are you.'

She could have said no again. She could have

turned her head away. But she did neither of those things. If anything she tilted her chin at him, meeting him in the moment he put his mouth to hers.

For a split-second old instincts surfaced and she stiffened, her body screaming its rejection. But the pressure of his mouth changed immediately. He softened, eased, and ultimately coaxed until her eyes closed. In the velvety blackness it was as if she'd been drugged and was now drowning in a warmth of sensation and bliss. His hands drifted delightfully, sweeping up her back—*holding* her but not forcing her against him. No, *she* was the one who pressed closer.

Muscles… Yes, she'd known he had muscles. But never in her life had she wanted to rub against a man the way she did now. Without thinking, almost without realising, she opened her mouth. His tongue slid between her parted lips, stroking lightly, teasing, before pulling back to trace the full pout of her lower lip. She felt the gentle throb of her pulse there, so highly sensitised she almost moaned. His lips covered hers again and his tongue strayed deeper—piercing, stroking the cavern of her mouth. She mewled as he caressed her more gently, more intimately than any man had. Licking. Sucking. Taking.

Her response was so sudden, so profound, that she began to tremble. Her fingers curled against the fine cotton of his shirt. She could feel the heat of him through the fabric. The heat that melded with her own. Something shifted deep inside her. Something irrevocable. And overwhelming.

It was a kiss unlike any other she'd experienced. Those other few had been sloppy or hard, and always quick, because they'd simply left her cold. This was anything but cold.

A great wave of sensation welled within her until she literally rose with it—reaching up onto her tiptoes, blindly stretching her arms over his shoulders, locking her hands about his neck, holding him as close as he held her. She flattened her breasts against his hard chest—her full, heavy breasts, with their achingly tight nipples—and the friction against his unyielding strength was devastating.

Something else swirled—a new kind of hunger that pushed her to rock her hips against his. She moaned as he immediately held her with stronger hands. Every cell in her body sang as he braced himself to absorb the strain of her body and she writhed with her need to get closer still to his hard strength. He sealed his mouth to hers again and he held her hips to grind against her.

For the first time in her life, Kassie had only one word in her mind, chanting over and over.

More.

More. More. More...

CHAPTER THREE

'YOUR HIGHNESS—'

The door opened and Giorgos released her so quickly Kassie almost fell. Instantly his hand shot out and gripped her arm to support her. His grip was hard. So were his eyes—like banked furnaces—and his gaze lasered through her. Assessing. *Judging.*

Dazed, she could see his thoughts racing. But she had no idea how the man could possibly *think* after experiencing that…that…

She recovered her balance in another moment and surreptitiously tugged her arm free, fighting to catch her breath quietly. Mortification flooded her. She'd just been caught in the King's arms like some shameless courtesan. But at the same time the interruption was welcome, because she had no idea where that might have gone if they hadn't been broken apart like that. She'd never done that or felt that—she'd been right to be wary of him. He was dangerous. And fascinating.

Sensation swirled around her body and embarrassment blushed over every inch of her skin. She realised the King was still staring at her, a thunderstruck expression on his face.

'I apologise, Your Highness, but we have found—'

'What?' He whirled away to bark at the man.

'These were hidden in the Princess's wardrobe.' The man held out some fabric and what looked like a knotted blue wig.

From the frown on his face it was clearly something Giorgos recognised. Kassie suspected the truth now—*the woman in the blue wig*—Eleni's disguise.

'Leave it on the table,' Giorgos snapped. 'And close the door behind you.'

The man's face was completely blank as he swiftly left the room.

'You're searching her private things?' Kassie whipped up her scorn, desperate to put space between them.

'My sister is missing,' he seethed. 'Of course I am searching her rooms for clues. I'll do whatever I have to do to find her.'

Her pulse thundered. 'And that's what that kiss

was?' He'd thought he could seduce her into spilling all the secrets she didn't even hold?

'Sorry—was I too gentle? You wanted the chains?' He suddenly smiled—a wicked, dangerous smile, as if he knew something she didn't. '*You're* the one fixated on becoming my prisoner. You know what that tells me about you?'

She glared at him. She didn't want to know what he thought of her now. She just wanted to get out of here—immediately—so she could try to assess and control the incoherent emotions coursing through her body.

'You obviously know everything. Doubtless you've read some dossier...'

'Actually, there was a lot left out,' he drawled.

He *truly* had a file on her? For how long had he been prying into her life? 'What *have* you learned?'

'You're the only child of Petra Marron. Your father is John Gale—though he doesn't acknowledge you as his daughter. You grew up in a small village an hour north of Palisades city. You excelled at school, and studied for your physiotherapy degree part-time after your mother became unwell with cancer. Upon graduation you took a job at the hospital and have been there ever since.

Your employment record is exemplary. Your patients speak highly of you. But your social media accounts don't show much in the way of relationships.'

She trembled, outraged by his physical and emotional invasion of her life and his ensuing obvious judgement. 'Perhaps I like my privacy and choose not to broadcast the details of my life to everyone.'

'Aren't you lucky to even have that choice?'

As if she were about to start feeling sorry for *him*! Her life had been reduced to a few sparse paragraphs, making it sound dull and unexciting, when in reality it had been rich and rewarding and heartbreaking.

'And what do you think you've learned from that collection of facts?'

'I already know you're not as perfect as that piece of paper makes you appear,' he said softly. 'I know you're not honest. I know you're deceptive, And I know you use your looks to—'

'To what? Seduce men into doing what I want?' She laughed, bitterly hurt by his unfounded accusations and assumptions.

She'd *never* used her looks—quite the opposite. She'd fought to be taken seriously—not to be tainted by preconceived opinions based on the shape of her body and the actions of her mother. And he was the worst of all—accusing her of hurting Eleni in some way.

But it was the blistering betrayal of her own body right now that appalled her. Scornful tears stung her eyes. 'Newsflash, Your Highness—here's some truth for you,' she snapped. *'I don't like to be touched.'*

She stilled at the look of shocked disbelief on his face, then shook her head, backing up as he stepped near her again. 'And that *wasn't* a challenge.'

But she'd read his frown of intent and the awful thing was that it wasn't honesty she wanted now, but his touch. That hidden part of her—dormant all her damn life—had been roused. But instead of being pleased about it, it terrified her.

'Not a challenge?' he questioned, and then he muttered grimly, 'Not the truth.'

She lashed out, trying the only way she could to push him away. 'I am *nobody's* precious thing. Certainly not to the half-brother I barely know. You will hurt no one but yourself. You'll get no revenge here. Only a stain on your soul. Sorry to disappoint you.'

'A stain on my soul?' Giorgos laughed equally bitterly.

Did she think he'd kissed her out of some medieval quest for vengeance on her family? Have mercy! It had taken only one second for him to lose his head completely when he'd got his hands on her heaven-sent curves.

'When you take advantage,' she clarified. 'When you exercise power over another just to make yourself feel good.'

Her bitterness made his skin shrivel with shame. Because for a moment there that was exactly what he'd wanted to do. Slake his anger and his frustration by satisfying himself with her beautiful body beneath his. Even now raw, desperate lust racked him in a shiver he could hardly contain—and he was furious with himself.

'Eleni is pregnant,' he gritted, goaded by guilt into revealing the terrible truth to her.

'What?' She paled. 'And you think Damon has taken her?'

He watched her. 'I don't believe she left willingly.'

But even as he said it, his sister's words echoed in his mind. *'I'm not coming back... Not till I've sorted it out.'*

'What does he want to do?'

'Apparently he's prepared to marry her.'

Relief bloomed in her face.

It only sharpened his anger. 'You think this is a *good* thing?'

'Maybe she cares about him. Maybe they're actually in love.'

'Maybe this is a fairy tale,' he growled derisively. 'Eleni is naive. If she does think she's in love with him it's because he's seduced her. He's conned her into believing it.'

'You're not going to give her any credit, are you?' Kassiani said, almost sadly. 'In your world she's just too innocent and too sweet and *too stupid* to make a decision on her own.' She suddenly flared up at him. 'Could you be *any* more insulting? No wonder she ran away. Either way, you're not going to believe her. Either he kidnapped her against her will or she went willingly because he bamboozled her. Because you think she's a brainless idiot. I bet you *totally* bully her.'

Giorgos blinked at her sudden snap. He didn't bully Eleni—she'd been happy with the arrangements he'd made…hadn't she? His stomach bottomed out. If she was happy, why wasn't she safe at home here in the palace? Was this woman right?

Had he underestimated Eleni's ability to make her own decisions? He needed to talk to her. But how could he?

He hadn't had a proper conversation with her in years.

The truth whispered, tormenting him. Guilt at his ineptitude curled, squeezing the air from his lungs. He'd thought he was doing the right thing. Maybe he'd been wrong all along. *Again.*

'My sister is in trouble,' he said starkly. 'All I want to do is help her. Help me help her.'

He heard her raggedly drawn in breath and saw the trembling of her mouth as she finally realised how desperate he was feeling.

'There's nothing I can say,' she said dully. 'Truthfully, I only met Damon a few years ago. He offered to help me.'

'Why?'

She hesitated before answering. 'He's a more genuine man than our father is. He's more caring. He'll want to do what he thinks is *right*.' She looked at him. 'He will want to protect both her and his unborn child.' A sad, twisted little smile curved her lush mouth. 'In a way, I feel sorry for the Princess. Between the two of you she's going to have quite a tough time.'

Giorgos stilled. Damon Gale was *protective*? He was not going to repeat the mistakes of his father? Kassiani was an illegitimate love-child. The abandoned daughter of an abandoned lover. Damon wasn't going to do that to his own child.

Perhaps his meeting with Eleni *hadn't* been contrived. Certainly on paper it seemed Damon Gale didn't need money or fame. In fact he actively sought privacy, as did his half-sister. So if his seduction of Eleni was by fate rather than some Machiavellian manipulation then Damon was only doing what he felt he had to. And if Giorgos was in the same position he had to admit he'd have done the same thing. Hell, a decade before he'd tried to.

He breathed out a long sigh, accepting that he was going to have to break the news to Eleni's fiancé that the planned wedding was off. He was going to have to back his sister. He was going to have to trust her.

He glanced up and saw Kassiani looking at him directly. Such sweet torment, standing only an arm's length away, watching him with a concerned look in her eyes. A concern that he hadn't earned.

His gut tightened as desire rose again.

No, neither concern nor pity was what he wanted from this woman. And that was wrong too.

'I want to go home,' she said softly.

Giorgos instinctively shook his head, instantly rejecting the idea of her departure. 'You can't. You know too much.'

'I won't breathe a word to anyone. Not to protect you but for your sister, who is kind and intelligent and funny and perfectly capable of making her own decisions.' She paused, her pout becoming pronounced. 'How you two can be related is beyond me.'

'You're not going home tonight,' he muttered as need speared through his body.

He wanted her to remain locked in the palace with him—to have her within his control. The remnants of his desire to punish her had now morphed into the fantasy of pleasuring her. Of seeing her aroused and begging for release. He could do it—he could please her. And in doing so please himself.

It had definitely been too long. And she… She *didn't like to be touched…*

He gritted his teeth, holding back a growl. Maybe he *was* no better than some twelfth-century warlord, taking a pretty captive to suit his pleasure—every bit the bastard she'd painted him. But right now he didn't care. He just wanted to forget everything in hedonistic pleasure.

He knew he could. He knew she'd liked his kiss. She'd wanted more. It would take little to make her want more again. Her molten chocolate eyes were now almost entirely black and he was losing himself in their bottomless depths.

'I'm not staying here,' she uttered in the faintest whisper.

Because she knew it too—knew that acting on this electricity arcing between them was inevitable. That was why she wanted to run away.

'You say you don't like to be touched,' he challenged her. 'But you enjoyed my touch. Not at first, sure. I took you by surprise, and I apologise for that, but don't lie about what happened then.'

The thought that he might have disgusted her was appalling. That he might have subjected her to something she had felt repulsive. Her reaction initially had been stiff, but he'd dismissed it as surprise because suddenly the floodgates had opened and she'd been ardent in her response.

And as he watched her closely now, as he listened to her, he saw other signs—the brightness of her eyes, the frantic beat of the pulse at her neck, the way she kept licking those lips that were obviously dry and bothering her. He remembered the way she'd softened and opened up for him. That hadn't been a moment he'd forced—that had been a moment of her surrender. Not to his will, but to the emotion flooding her. The desire for deeper touch.

She'd been attracted to him. She still was. But she didn't want to be. And perhaps he could understand why.

'Someone hurt you,' he said. His anger lit again, but this time in a different way.

She frowned at him searchingly, then rolled her eyes. 'Not in the way you're thinking.'

'No one has touched you when you didn't want them to?' He didn't believe her.

'They have. But I stopped them.'

He lifted his brows.

'It wasn't about control or anything worse.' Her colour rose. 'I just mean a kiss at the end of a date…'

'How did you stop him?'

'Men don't like a lover who doesn't respond. No matter the attributes she might have.'

He shook his head. She knew her 'attributes' were like catnip to any red-blooded man. But he knew there'd be some men out there who wouldn't care about whether she responded to them or not. Those men would just take—in which case she'd been lucky. But her lack of response was… *interesting.*

'You didn't respond to them?' He felt very still inside.

'As I said, I don't like to be touched.' She folded her arms, looking like a spiky ball of defensiveness.

Did she mean she didn't feel anything at all? Or she just hadn't met a guy who could actually push her buttons? 'Are you saying you're frigid?'

That flush covered her skin and he watched her as she refused to answer. He realised now it was the truth—or at least she thought it was.

'You don't feel things that way?' He framed the question more gently.

For a second he didn't know whether to believe her or whether this was another game. But then, she hadn't been playing any game at all, had she? She hadn't known a thing about Eleni and Damon.

He thought about the doctor who'd asked her for a date this evening. Her refusal had been polite and firm and *practised.* That nurse had teased her, but she'd stepped in and helped her deflect the guy's attention as if she'd known it made Kassie uncomfortable. And there'd been a stiffness within her when she'd first met him. Now her lips were still clamped shut, but he could see the trembling of her body.

'It's *not* a challenge.'

Her voice was low and husky and he could feel the mortification emanating from her. She clearly wished like hell she'd not said anything.

'I don't take it as one,' he reassured her. But then he smiled. 'I don't need to prove something I already know.'

She looked confused.

'You felt "that way" when I kissed you.'

She shifted and her skin flooded again with deepened colour. Her gaze dropped from his. 'Please don't embarrass yourself.'

His laughter was husky and amused. 'Kassie…' He'd heard the nurse call her that—he liked it.

'Please.' She closed her eyes. 'I don't see why it's all that amusing.'

'It's not that it's funny. I'm relieved.' He leaned close. 'I didn't want to think I'd hurt you that way. Contrary to your earlier assumption, I *don't* get off on forcing my attentions on unwilling women.'

'I know that. I'm sure they're all very, *very* willing.'

She still wouldn't look at him. But he couldn't look away from her. 'Right now I'm only interested in you. And I think you're willing.'

'No,' she denied.

'Be honest,' he dared her softly. 'Sometimes you can't help who you're attracted to. Even if you don't like the person, chemistry can be just chemistry.'

'But you *can* choose whether to act on that attraction or not,' she said crisply.

'So you admit there's attraction?' He smiled. She was thawing fractionally. 'You're used to choosing not to act. Maybe you're used to choosing to *avoid*. Not because you *can't* feel, but because you're afraid to.'

She shook her head vehemently. 'You're wrong.'

'I don't think so,' he said. 'Aren't you in the least bit curious?'

She rolled her eyes again, but it lost the desired effect because he could see how her fingers were trembling.

'It's not something I need,' she said.

Didn't *everyone* need touch sometimes? Even he did—in the strictly controlled liaisons he occasionally permitted himself. But if she was being honest then Kassiani Marron's confession had just eliminated her from contention for one of those brief, discreet dalliances.

'The conversation is only academic,' he assured her quietly. 'The last thing I would do is touch you now. Or hurt you.'

'If you don't want to hurt me, then let me leave.'

For another fleeting second he questioned whether she was truly as innocent as those wide eyes would lead him to believe. He'd been lied to by a beautiful woman before.

But then he remembered the shocked stillness of her body when he'd been foolish enough to touch her when he shouldn't have. The frankly inexpert answer of her kiss. And her reaction afterwards—the rapid rise and fall of her breasts as she'd worked to recover her breath, the trembling of her limbs. She'd been more than aroused. She'd been stunned. And she *was* being honest.

The realisation forced him to shut down all the burning want within his body. He was extremely cautious when selecting a lover and would never have an affair with a woman who was clearly fragile—no matter how beautiful she might be. Kassiani Marron was a risk he was unprepared to subject himself to. Duty forbade it. The past forbade it. And the past had already come back to haunt him.

His sister was now in a position he'd hoped to avoid for her. His interest in Kassie would have to be ignored. This night was nothing more than a moment that she would soon forget.

Kassie watched as his expression changed from intensely speculative to serious and then to blank. She felt his withdrawal of interest almost as a physical chill—and for once she felt regret at successfully putting a guy off.

'I'll ensure you get home safely,' he said as he stepped away from her.

'I'm sure your assistant will be very efficient.' She couldn't keep the coldness from her own tone.

He turned, catching her gaze with his. 'You know I'm escorting you myself.'

'You're just trying to find out more information.'

His sudden chuckle caught her by surprise.

'So suspicious,' he mocked. 'Are you this wary with everyone?'

'You're every bit as defensive as I am.'

'I think you already know you set me on edge, Ms Marron.'

And he didn't like it. That eased her own issues with his effect on *her*. 'It seems we're even.'

His laugh encircled her with a warm glow. The tension lifted for the briefest of moments and she couldn't hold back her answering smile. When he was like this he was the most incredibly attractive man. And now that she could relax a fraction she realised it was a *good* thing—to find a guy attractive? *Go her.*

Something flickered in his eyes before he mastered control of himself and became the serious monarch again. 'It really is time for you to leave.'

'Freedom. At last,' she muttered mock-demurely. 'Thank you, Your Highness.'

She heard a sharp intake of breath but he said nothing. He stalked ahead of her along the long dimly lit corridors, their gold detailing providing a muted gleam in the vast shadows. He was fascinating.

That unsettling feeling deep in her belly stirred again, spreading that strange ache. Once more she replayed that kiss—the shocking heat that had flooded her body surged again. *Desire.*

She almost stumbled as the need to feel his

body against hers again made her stupid muscles weaken.

'Truly, you don't need to accompany me.' She tried to deflect him as they emerged into the night. She might as well have tried pushing a marble slab up an icy slope.

'It's my duty to ensure you get home safely.'

'You don't trust your own security people?'

'It's my responsibility.'

That rebellious feeling flared again. '*I'm* not your responsibility.'

'Right now, your welfare is.'

The guy had an overblown hero complex, thinking himself responsible for anyone he thought was weaker or less able. He was determined to be the protector.

'The way your sister is your responsibility?'

He checked his stride, then kept walking. 'No. Not like that at all.'

He made a small gesture with his hand and the waiting security team by the car melted into the shadows. He held open the rear door and she got into the car. She watched as he walked around the vehicle to get in the other side, next to her.

The driver moved the car forward the moment he'd closed the door. The palace gates slid open and they swiftly glided through the dark, quiet streets. She stared ahead blindly, hyper-aware of his gaze on her.

The silence in the car thickened. The emotions swirling within her were too strong to contain—they leaked out, heating the atmosphere between her and the silent presence beside her. He was lethally powerful, yet she sensed that extreme protectiveness actually masked vulnerability. As arrogant and as privileged as he was, he was exposed because he loved his sister. He wanted what was best for her.

Kassie couldn't help but respect him for that. Because part of her wished *she'd* had someone who'd cared like that in her life. Someone who loved her and watched out for her. King Giorgos might be arrogant, but she understood that he wanted what was best for the ones he loved.

Fool, she mocked herself. One kiss and she was thinking herself half in love with the man already? The sooner she got away from him and back to her mundane, safe world the better.

But as the car pulled up to her small apartment she hesitated and turned to him. 'I won't say anything,' she promised in a low voice. 'You may not believe me, but I do want the best for Princess Eleni. And I understand that you do too.'

'I don't require your approval, Ms Marron. I will find Eleni and I will bring her home safely.'

He didn't like knowing she'd seen his vulnerability. She understood that too.

She licked her dry lips. 'I'm certain you will.'

He got out of the car at the same time she did. She veered away from him as she walked to her door, quickly trying to find her keys and unlock it, but her fingers had become buttery and useless.

'Thank you for bringing me home,' she said with mechanical politeness. 'I'm sorry I couldn't be of more assistance.'

His lips curved and that gleam lit in his eye again. 'Never apologise when you are not actually sorry.'

'I'm sorry that you're worrying,' she pointed out coolly. 'I wish there was something more I could do.'

He looked at her but didn't answer. For a moment that thing swirled between them again. The memory of his body pressed against hers flashed into her mind. The foreign sensation of delight sizzled deep in her blood cells, beating heat into her cheeks again. Her throat clogged. She couldn't speak again if she tried. Nor could she move.

He took one step nearer. Night shadowed his eyes and she couldn't read his expression. But she could feel it—the sharp edge of desire. Only in her inexperience, her naivety, she couldn't truly be certain that it was shared, or if it was only her crazy, out-of-control body.

He took the key from her useless fingers and stretched past her to unlock the door. She'd never felt as frozen as she did in that moment. But it wasn't ice immobilising her muscles. It was heat and want and an appalling sense of anticipation.

He regarded her closely. 'You'd better get inside, Ms Marron. Now. Before…'

He trailed off and she stared up at him.

'Before what?' she breathed.

He gazed down at her in silence for a long, long moment. But this time he didn't act on the impulse that had shocked them both. He gave a clipped nod and then he turned and strode into the darkness.

Kassie slowly entered the safety of her tiny apartment. As she locked the door she leaned back against it, accepting the reality that she would never see King Giorgos again.

And wasn't that good? He was arrogant and stubborn and saw only the worst in her. There was nothing in common between them.

But she pressed a hand against her ribs, willing away the ache. His departure from her life shouldn't bring any sense of loss. Yet it did. Which meant she was more broken than even she'd believed.

CHAPTER FOUR

I DON'T LIKE to be touched.

Her words haunted him. Not a challenge—no, Giorgos had no desire to overpower her. But he did have a duty to warn her, because she wouldn't like being hunted either. And she was about to be.

Keeping Eleni and Damon clear of the paparazzi's long-range lenses was easy enough, but Ms Marron had none of the palace's defences at her disposal. He was not having anyone else suffering because of the burden of the crowns that he and Eleni wore.

Half an hour before the announcement was due to be made he went to her apartment. It was less than two days since he'd met her. But he'd spent too many minutes thinking about her and he knew she wasn't going to welcome his reappearance.

There was no reply to his forceful knock on her door. It took his security man only a moment to pick the feeble lock.

'Wait for me out here,' he ordered as he stepped inside.

'Sir…?'

He glanced back to silence the man with a look.

Her apartment was small but cosy—there were books stacked on an old table, a pot plant on the windowsill was flowering, and the room had a sense of comfort. But one of the window fastenings was loose and in her bedroom the curtains were too thin. The sight of her neatly made narrow bed tightened his skin.

She wouldn't be safe here and it was his responsibility to ensure her safety. *He* was the one responsible for the mess they were now in. He clamped down on the searing satisfaction he felt at the thought of having her with him again. This was for *her* benefit, not his. *Her* protection. And he'd prove to himself that his full control was restored.

'Pack her a bag for a few days,' he said to the waiting guard as he strode out of the small unit.

He swallowed his guilt about invading her personal space—hell, he was used to living with guilt. She'd be furious, but too bad. She was too vulnerable to remain there for the foreseeable future.

He quickly slid into the unmarked car idling at the kerb. 'The hospital,' he instructed his driver. 'As fast as you can without drawing attention.'

Kassie's pulse kept skipping beats in a maddeningly unpredictable rhythm. She'd barely slept these last two nights. When she was alone in her little apartment the memories teased and that sweltering heat returned. The recollections were too intense, too intimate. She'd curl up in a ball and squeeze her eyes tight shut to block them, but it didn't work. Cold showers hadn't worked either.

Why did fate have to be so fickle? Why was it that the one man who'd ever turned her on was the one she could never have? The one she'd never actually want?

The only way to stop those thoughts was by distracting herself with her patients and paperwork. She'd worked on her files all afternoon, stopping briefly to snack on a sandwich from the vending machine on the second floor.

Now, as she was on her way back through the ward to her office, she saw one of her patients in distress.

'It's sore?'

She felt for this youth who'd sustained a crush

injury; they were trying to prevent an amputation. The boy was tearful, but she kept talking to him quietly as she carefully massaged the area above the damage, taking care not to inflame it.

'Thanks.'

She smiled at him gently. 'It's going to take time. Don't try to do too much too soon. It's easy to make that mistake.'

She stepped out from behind the curtain to go back to her office and her stressed heart stopped beating altogether. King Giorgos was standing right on the other side of the curtain, immaculate as always in another impeccable suit.

'You're eavesdropping?' she whispered furiously. 'Have you no respect for *anyone's* privacy?' She hurried to get out of earshot of the other patients. 'What are you *doing* here?'

'What are *you* doing here?' King Giorgos countered lazily, walking with her. 'You're not rostered on this weekend.'

She gaped at him. How did he *know* that? 'I needed to complete the paperwork I didn't finish the other night.'

'That wasn't paperwork.'

'He was in pain—you expect me to ignore him?'

She shook her head and snapped at him tartly. 'I'm sorry—I'm not like you.'

His mouth flattened. 'You must come with me now.'

'I can't leave. I have to work.'

'It's cancelled for the week.'

The week? The ground shifted beneath her feet. 'Why?'

'Because your life is about to get crazy.' He glanced into her office. 'Get your bag. You're coming with me now.'

'This again?' She folded her arms and glared at him. 'Is your life incomplete without a captive? Must you always have a female in chains in the palace?'

A sharply amused gleam softened his stern expression. 'You really *do* have a fixation with me putting you in chains, don't you?'

A trickle of something delicious and dangerous seeped into her. Engaging with him like this gave her a thrill she'd never have believed she'd actively seek.

'I'm doing this for your protection, Ms Marron. Not for your pleasure. Or mine,' he said pointedly. 'A helicopter is waiting on the roof.'

She stopped walking. 'You can't be serious.'

'And *you* can't be this naive. They're already on their way.'

'They?'

'Journalists, cameramen, paparazzi, vultures. Whatever you want to call them.'

'Why would they want to bother *me*?'

'They are going to touch you,' he warned her grimly. 'They are going to pry.'

'I don't care what they write about me.' She held herself stiffly. It couldn't be anything worse than she'd heard over the years.

He looked pityingly at her. 'It's not what they write—it is the way they follow you…stalk you, harass you, call out to you. They'll speak to anyone you've ever spoken to in your life… You need to get away—at least until the initial furore dies down.'

He walked to the door leading to the stairwell, expecting her to follow him.

The desire to flout his demand flared. 'You can't be—'

'Move,' he ordered curtly. 'Or I'll carry you up there myself.'

His threat merely sharpened her urge for insubordination.

'You just can't cope with someone who doesn't

instantly submit to your demands, can you?' She defied him with an all-out assault. 'You expect everyone to bow and scrape and scuttle to do your bidding. Especially women. Do you kit out all your lovers with a set of knee-pads?'

He froze, but his eyes lit with such danger she thought she might have gone too far. Where had her aggression come from? The instinct to push back had been irresistible, but she'd never been *shrewish* before.

'What?' she asked, faking bravado. 'Did I strike too close to home?'

He tugged her into the stairwell and slammed the door behind them. 'You are *so* determined to provoke a reaction in me,' he whispered, hemming her in against the cool wall with his hands. 'So keen to make me lash out in a specific way.'

He leaned closer still.

'You want me to do what I did the other night so you can cast me as your villain. But the truth is you liked it. You're attracted to me. You want me. You just don't want to admit it.' His lips curved with arrogant satisfaction.

'I don't want you.'

Her heart thundered. She was shocked at his verbal attack. Shocked more by the unfurling betrayal of her body. He was right. She *did* want him.

His gaze swept down, lingering on her tightened breasts.

She gasped. 'You're the most arrogant creature who walked the planet.'

'Well, that's a step up from being a monster.' He laughed. 'And at least I'm honest.'

'You want honesty?'

'It'd be a good start.'

'You're the *last* man I'd be attracted to.'

He snorted. 'I think I'm the *only* man you have been attracted to.'

He was right—which was all the more annoying. Why did it have to be *him*, of all people?

'Everything comes too easily to you,' she grumbled. 'You think you can have any woman you want. Everything in your life is disposable.'

'*Nothing* in my life is disposable.' His smile gained a bitter edge. 'Everything I do has more consequences than for most people. Nothing is forgotten.' He stepped back but took her clenched fist in his hand. 'Did some powerful, wealthy man hurt you, Kassiani?'

Of course. Starting with her louse of a father.

'What makes you think there was only one?'

'Poor little thing… But the pity card isn't going to work on me,' he muttered, unmoved. 'Your past isn't my problem. I'm concerned only with now. And right now you need to come with me.'

'And if I refuse?'

'You just want me to toss you over my shoulder.' He laughed again at her expression. 'Do you think I wouldn't dare?'

She stared up at him. He would. But she couldn't give in this easily—especially considering he was the one man she found sexually attractive.

'I am trying to save you from a horror-fest,' he growled.

'I can take care of myself.'

He released her fist with a theatrical sigh and dug into his pocket.

'Take a look at the damn screen.' He flicked his phone around, almost shoving the screen in her face. 'This is the mob outside your apartment right now.'

There was a bunch of men standing around outside her apartment. Guys in jeans and tees on scooters, with cameras and lights and phones. One was repeatedly banging on her door.

'How can you see my apartment?' She frowned. 'Have you put cameras on me?'

'This is a live feed from my security team. I have someone stationed in the building across the street to keep an eye on the place and the other is…' He swiped the screen again, fury flickering across his face as he checked the screen before showing her again. 'You can't go home. Not until I have this under control.'

Kassie stared at the grainy image on the screen. There were two guys right in her back yard. 'They're going through my *rubbish*?' Appalled, she leaned back against the cool wall for support. 'That's sick.'

'*Now* do you understand? You don't want to be running that gauntlet. You don't want to hear their questions and have their cameras in your face. You need to leave with me. Now. They'll already be here at the hospital, trying to get through Security.'

'Why are they even here?' She was shocked—she didn't understand it at all.

'Because your half-brother has just married my sister.'

She gaped at him for a full five seconds.

'What?' she muttered breathlessly. 'He's what?'

'They returned. They married. This afternoon.'

She registered the grim tension in his eyes. 'Are they okay? Is Eleni okay?'

'I think so.' Uncertainty flickered across his face, but then he straightened. 'More okay than *you're* about to be if you don't come with me now.'

And was Giorgos okay? Because, to be honest, he didn't really look it. He looked pale and, frankly, right on the edge.

Wordlessly, she turned and walked up the stairs with him, so full of questions that she didn't know where to begin.

Less than two minutes later she was strapped in to take the first helicopter ride of her life. Giorgos handed her a headset and she put it on with fumbling fingers as the machine lifted into the sky.

'We have a secure channel.' His voice sounded too close, too intimate, even though he sat a foot apart from her in his own surprisingly spacious seat. 'Not even the pilot can hear us.'

Yeah? Well she wasn't about to have headset sex with him. She was too busy clutching on to the armrest and remembering to breathe, trying to get her head around the developments of the last ten minutes.

'Are you okay?' he asked, a reluctant smile breaking his frown.

'I'm fine. You?'

'I will be.' He shot her a look. 'I'm sorry.'

So was she. Because there was scandal here. Her mother had been a mistress—the 'other woman'. And she was a child born of lust. The exact sort of juicy scandal that royals ought never to be tainted with…

'How do you cope with it?' She gestured to the phone he still held. 'How do you live with that level of intrusion?'

'I don't have to. They don't scrutinise me the way they would you or any woman.' He frowned. 'I know it's not right. That's why…'

'You never have a girlfriend? You'd never subject any woman to this.'

'I can't protect anyone from it.' He sighed. 'Someone born into the craziness understands it, and at least has built the defences to cope with it. But the women get it far worse than the men.'

'This is why you're so protective of Eleni?' It made sense to her now.

'I've seen what it does to other women in public positions. I've seen their skeletal figures and the strain on their made-up faces at the stress of having their dress choices stupidly picked apart.' He shoved his phone back into his pocket. 'I didn't want that for her. *Ever.* I wanted her out of the spotlight as much as possible. To go from the safety of one palace to another.'

'But you can't hide her away from life.'

'Obviously not,' he said grimly. 'She was too vulnerable and naive.'

'Because she hadn't been out there—living life like a normal young woman, making mistakes—'

'That was impossible,' he argued strongly. But then he sighed. 'And now she's made the oldest mistake in the world…'

'So you've made Damon marry her?'

'I don't think I could make him do anything he didn't want to—he's *your* half-brother after all.' He shot her a look. 'He all but abducted Eleni to prevent her marrying Prince Xander. *He's* the one who pushed for this. Eleni thought she could go it alone.'

'And you don't think she could?' Kassie felt her fighting spirit stir. 'My mother went it alone.'

'And was it easy?'

'Of course not, but—'

'Then you know exactly why I didn't want that for Eleni,' he interjected. 'But it was Damon, not me, who convinced Eleni that marriage was the best answer. I wasn't the bully this time—it had already happened.'

His gaze narrowed on her thoughtfully.

'And how was it for you?' he asked quietly.

'How was what?'

'Your mother's decision to go it alone?'

'She didn't really have a choice, given my father was already married,' she muttered through gritted teeth. 'She avoided other men.'

'And she taught you too well. You avoid *all* men.'

'Do you blame me?' she flared. 'I watched my mother wait and wait and wait for her lover to deliver what he promised. She settled for second-best for so long, taking someone else's crumbs her entire life. And for what? Lies and rejection and heartache and sickness.'

'She wasn't ever interested in anyone else?'

'Because getting another man is all that matters?' Kassie was incensed.

'I imagine there were many men interested in your mother.'

'Because all a man wants is a beautiful woman?'

'*Must* you interpret my questions so simply? I'm quite certain your mother had multiple attractive qualities. Intelligence. Spirit. Determination. Compassion—'

'And you're certain of this—?'

'Because her daughter shows the same things, of course.'

She didn't know quite how to respond to that. He was mercurial. Shockingly honest. Suave. Dangerous.

'But you're determined not to be the same as her,' he said.

Kassie stiffened. 'I loved my mother…' And she was loyal to her, even though she'd frustrated Kassie so much. And hurt her.

'Of course.'

'They're really married?' She couldn't believe it.

He pulled out his phone again, turning it so she could see the picture he'd opened. Her heart softened at the sight of her half-brother and the Princess. Laughing, close. Their connection would be obvious to anyone who looked. Perhaps it was going to work out.

'They look happy.'

'Appearances can be deceptive—'

'No.' Kassie pointed at the sparkle in Eleni's eyes and her glowing smile. 'You can't fake that.'

He didn't answer as he studied the photo again.

'I don't know Damon well,' she admitted with full disclosure. 'But I *do* know he's a far better man than our father has ever been. Damon's a *good* man.'

'Only time will tell,' Giorgos answered quietly.

He didn't trust people. She supposed he must have reason—just as she had reason.

'Where are you taking me?' she asked.

'The Summer House.'

The royal holiday retreat? She shifted on her seat, her gaze sliding from his.

'Eleni and Damon need space alone at the palace,' he said calmly. 'You need to get away from the intrusiveness of the paparazzi. And I can continue to work there.'

'So it's convenient for you?'

'When did you last have a holiday?' he cajoled with a glint in his eye. 'When did you last spoil yourself? You've spent all your adult life either caring for your mother or studying so you can care for others. You deserve a break.'

'Are you implying that I ought to *thank* you? As if you're doing me a *favour*? This isn't my dream holiday.' She suddenly choked on a laugh. 'And you think you're not arrogant!'

He grinned smugly. 'Look out of the window now. I think you'll find it's not so bad.'

She finally braved a glance down to the coastline. It was a stunning island—fertile gardens, impressive rock formations and aquamarine waters. She saw a low building, growing larger as they neared it. Set into the cliff, it almost formed part of the rocks itself.

She gazed at it as they circled to the rear of the building, where there was a helipad. The windows gleamed but the silence of the place astonished her. There were no crowds of attendants. No other buildings nearby.

She walked with him—initially wary—but the Summer House was nothing like the palatial monstrosity in the city.

It was large, but not vast or ostentatious. Where there were overly ornate gold decorations in the palace, there was white simplicity here. There were no paintings smothering every wall, or chandeliers hanging from the ceilings, or sculptures and furniture crammed into every corner. No, here there was pale, honey-coloured flooring, and white walls, and luxurious space and a sense of serenity so profound that the power of speech was stolen from her.

It truly was beautiful. And private. More than that, it was *intimate.*

'It's built into an existing cave network. Above us there's a garden—not large, but private. And there's a pool that's partially inside a cave, partially in the sun.'

'It's…' She wasn't too proud to be honest. 'It's not what I expected. It's much simpler.'

Warm and restful and so beautifully light and fresh she just knew all those soft furnishings were the most luxuriant one could get.

'I knew you'd like it.' His smile flashed—but it wasn't that arrogantly satisfied one, there was genuine pleasure in his eyes. 'Not as formal as the palace.'

'No.'

Kassie's heart thudded as something darkly sweet slipped beneath her guard. He'd *wanted* her to like it. He'd wanted to please her.

That sense of cosy intimacy grew. The night was closing in, the brilliant blue sky swiftly darkening with each passing second, and Kassie's awareness deepened. She was now alone with him—effectively trapped here with him for who knew how long.

A shiver ran along her spine.

Not a thrill of anticipation. It couldn't possibly be that.

She ought to be outraged by him taking her, but somehow his revelations on the helicopter ride had taken that particular wind from her sails.

'Are you hungry?' he asked.

She shook her head. 'I had a snack at the hospital.'

'Then I'll show you to your room so you can get comfortable.'

He led the way down a wide corridor. Where was his room? She didn't dare ask.

He waited for her to enter ahead of him. It was simply and sparsely decorated, with white walls, white furnishings and white linen on the wide, wide bed. Yet somehow it wasn't cold and impersonal—it was warm and inviting and too intimate for her to be in it alone with him. That intense feeling fluttered—and with it came that curl of fear.

'Is that my bag?' She stared poisonously at the small carry-all that had been placed on the hand-carved wooden rack at the end of that magnificent bed.

She whirled to face him, turning her back on the searing intimacy of the beautiful bedroom.

He stood impassively, not answering, his gaze not leaving her face.

'Did you go into my apartment? Did you pack my clothes?' She whipped her anger to ice.

He shook his head. 'One of my men packed.'

'So some random guy I've never met has raided my underwear drawer?'

He cleared his throat. 'I thought you would prefer to have your own things rather than accept an entirely new wardrobe paid for by me. Especially not underwear.'

He was right about that, of course. But he was still wrong. The outrageously high-handed behaviour was shocking, and she was seized by the desire to better him.

'Whatever made you think that?' she asked brazenly. 'What woman *wouldn't* love a selection of new dresses and shoes and, yes, underwear to waft about a place like this in? Especially if she didn't have to pay for it.'

He blinked, but then a slow smile spread across his face. 'Don't worry,' he soothed. 'If you're that upset about me not seeing your underwear you can show it to me yourself later.'

There was a pregnant pause as she read the searing challenge in his eyes. The ripple of banter brewed into brooding resistance. She couldn't tear her gaze from his—was locked in a moment of intensity. His magnetism was overwhelming. She almost needed to glue her feet to the floor to stop herself walking towards him.

'I'm not sleeping with you,' she muttered low.

'Did I offer?' he replied, his gaze still not leaving her.

She flushed, but continued with her deflection because she *had* to solidify her position. 'We're practically related. You're—what? My brother-in-law now?'

'I'm not *any* kind of brother to you,' he said softly. 'Not even close.'

'You're standing close.'

Somehow he was. Somehow in the past few minutes he'd got close enough to block out everything else in the world. Close enough for her to feel his heat.

He reached out, carefully brushing back a lock of hair that had escaped her braid. '*Not* brotherly,' he muttered huskily.

'I… I get that.' She swallowed, suddenly sweltering.

'Then I'll leave you to unpack.' He stepped back. 'Rest. Swim if you like. If you need anything just ask one of the staff. The few that are here are my most trusted employees and they'll get whatever you need. Please feel at home here.'

He *had* to be kidding. This place was small to him, but larger and more luxurious than any home *she'd* lived in. But she couldn't help exploring her room. There were two other rooms attached—a gorgeous sitting room, with a sofa and a comfy armchair and a wide set of windows leading to a balcony overlooking the water. And then there was the bathroom.

She caught sight of her reflection in the gleaming mirrors and almost died. But she turned her back on the large bath—she couldn't quite relax enough for that. She'd freshen up in that magnificent shower.

The jets of water were sublime. The soaps and shampoos deliciously scented. The towels soft and fluffy and, yes, she was lost to decadence for a good half-hour. But as she dressed in the jeans and tee shirt that had been folded with annoying perfection into her bag she wondered what he expected her to do—if anything.

She quickly re-tied her braid and decided. She refused to hide in her suite and wait to be summoned into his presence…

But, despite the simplicity of the house, it proved to be larger than she'd initially thought. The curving corridors confused her—it really *was* built into a cave network and it really *was* utterly divine.

On her way back from another dead-end corridor that had led to that incredible pool he'd mentioned, a sleekly attired man met her.

'May I help you, miss?'

'I'm just looking for the King.'

The man's eyes widened slightly as he glanced down and noticed her bare feet. 'If you'd like to wait, I can tell him you're looking for him.'

She saw she'd missed a corridor off to the left, and from there she could hear soft music playing. 'There's no need—I can tell him myself. He's down there?'

The man didn't deny it, and didn't stop her, but he did look alarmed.

'Don't worry.' She smiled at him.

She didn't bother knocking—just opened the door and walked in.

'You've been prowling around?'

Giorgos was sprawled back on a large sofa, his tie askew, his shirtsleeves rolled up and a dangerous gleam in his eyes. A silver platter of delicacies sat on a low table in front of him—olives, meats, breads—all untouched as far as she could tell. The bottle of whisky next to the platter, however, had definitely been touched, and the amber liquid more than half filled the crustal tumbler he was holding.

'Looking for your private lair.' She nodded. 'It seems I've finally found it.'

'I like the door shut.' His hot gaze lingered on the dampened ends of her braid and he took a long sip of his drink.

Kassie held her breath as she closed the door and turned back to face him. Playing with fire was for fools, and she was afraid she might be the biggest fool of them all. And yet she couldn't quite walk away.

'Is your room to your satisfaction?' he asked in a mockery of civility.

'I suppose it will do,' she mused slowly as she perched on the distant arm of the sofa he was sitting on.

'Maintaining your reputation of being difficult to please?' He quirked an eyebrow at her. But his hint of a smile faded the longer he gazed at her. 'I'm tired, Kassie,' he suddenly blurted out roughly. 'I don't want to do the right thing. I want to do everything I shouldn't. If you don't want me to do that then you need to walk away right now. *Please.*'

She cocked her head and looked at him closely, realising that beneath that in-control demeanour there was a man who was tired and hurting. And alone.

'You're upset.'

'I'm hard,' he argued bluntly. 'I'm tired and I want to lose myself in sex. I want to kiss you until you sigh and spread your legs and let me plunge as deep as I can into you. And I'm not sorry if I'm shocking you. I'm being honest about why you need to leave the room. *Now.*'

She almost fell from her perch. His harshly expelled words *did* shock her. But she realised he'd intended them to. He wanted to scare her away because he didn't want to be seen like this. Because he was feeling vulnerable.

Too bad.

'As if you can't control yourself… I *know* you can.'

'But I don't want to,' he ground out. 'And that's when things get tricky. I'm ordering you to leave.'

'You were the one who dragged me here.' She

smiled serenely at him and let herself slip down off the wide arm onto the seat of the sofa.

He growled again and took another sip of his whisky.

'What will you do if I leave the room?' she asked.

He studied the contents of his glass. 'Continue to get drunk.'

'Is that your secret vice? How boring.'

'Are you calling me *boring*?' He leaned forward and set the glass on the low table in front of him. 'You're right, I am. I haven't got drunk in a decade.'

'So it won't take much, then, will it? Perhaps I'll need to save the kingdom from a king with a hangover? We don't want your legendary impartiality to be impaired. Perhaps I should stay and talk to you for a while.'

'You're determined to torment me,' he groaned and pressed his hands to his eyes. 'What did I do to deserve this fate?' He winced and muttered beneath his breath. 'Don't answer that—I already know.'

'You're the one who brought me here.'

He opened his eyes. 'And I'm going to regret it.'

'You think?' She laughed. 'We all want things we can't have.'

'Of course. There are many things I can't have. Many things Eleni didn't have. And that was *my* fault.'

'Are you wallowing in guilt and self-pity?'

'Utterly.' He picked up his glass again. 'I failed her.'

She heard the serious thread beneath that mocking tone and couldn't help but respond honestly. 'She's an adult. She's made her own choices. You have to let her get on with it.'

'I'm trying.'

'I know.' She smiled shyly at him. 'I also know it isn't easy when you're used to being in complete control.'

He looked at her sombrely. 'You would know.' There was no irony in his tone, no sarcasm.

But she shook her head and laughed. '*So* not the same. I can't get the career track I want. I can't—'

'I mean complete control of your *emotions*,' he interrupted. 'Of your body. You don't want distractions.' He reached out and took her hand. 'Yet you respond to me,' he said quietly.

She curled her fingers into a fist, but she couldn't lie to him. 'Apparently so.'

'Why do you think that is?'

She turned her gaze on the glass. 'Perhaps it's the power. Perhaps in that way I'm as weak as my mother.'

'She was attracted to a powerful man?'

'The most powerful she'd met. John Gale was handsome, intelligent. He promised the world and delivered nothing.'

'What happened?'

'Nothing. That was the point.' Her chuckle was bitter. 'He lied. He was greedy. He kept her enamoured for years. She put her life on hold for him. She jumped when he called. She always jumped…' Kassie trailed off, embarrassed.

'She loved him,' Giorgos said.

'It wasn't *love*.' Kassie frowned. 'She didn't love herself. She accepted too little from him.'

'And now you don't accept anything from any man?'

She shot him a look, but he shrugged and continued.

'You live alone…you're fiercely independent. And you don't date…'

'You've changed your view. You thought I'd slept with all the doctors,' she said pointedly.

'I'm sorry about that. I was worried about Eleni and I wasn't thinking clearly.'

'But you took one look at me and made up your mind.' She shook her head. 'Don't worry—you're not the first guy to do that.'

He sighed and reached forward to put his glass on the table again. He turned to face her. 'I'm sorry for that too. Is that part of why you don't want any kind of relationship?'

His apologies mollified her—and his honesty encouraged her own. 'It's not that I don't want a relationship—doesn't everyone want that special person? To be in love and be loved? It's that I don't *feel* any attraction. There's a difference.'

'Yet you feel attraction to me?'

She nodded. 'Isn't fate cruel?'

'Because I'm powerful?' He watched her. 'What if I had no power?' he asked softly. 'What if there was no crown, no palace, no Summer House…just an average man in a tee shirt and jeans. Would you still respond to me?'

Of course. Because his power wasn't to do with all those external things, it was an intrinsic part of him. And she responded on an equally intrinsic level.

'There is no point wondering "what if?" The

fact is you *are* the King, you *have* a crown and palaces and all the power.'

'So there can be nothing?'

'Exactly.'

'There could be this moment,' he tempted.

'Don't…' she whispered.

'There's no reason why we can't we enjoy each other's company.'

'There's *every* reason.'

She should have left when he'd told her to, but she'd thought she could remain immune to him and keep herself at a distance.

No, you didn't.

'There's every reason to steal a moment, Kassie,' he said softly, his expression revealing his awareness of her wavering contrary thoughts. 'Don't you deserve just a moment?'

'As if it would be *good* for me?' She rolled her eyes.

But that little voice of truth whispered, mocking. It *would* be good for her. And the heat unfurling in her depths was the real reason for staying when he had told her to go.

'I'd make it good.' He chuckled at the look she shot him. 'You know it's true. Why don't you let me try and we'll see how you like it?'

'As if I haven't heard that line before!'

'You already liked it a little. I think you might like it a lot.'

He scooted along the sofa until he sat the merest inch from her. Her skin sizzled and her pulse raced. Every cell yearned for him to come closer still. She refused to look at him.

'I could make you feel so good. You know that's true. I already make you feel.'

She swallowed hard. 'You're not being fair.'

'No.' He smiled at her. 'But life isn't fair.'

She looked into his eyes and the second she did so temptation screamed along her bones. 'Your H—'

'Call me Giorgos,' he gritted. 'I'm not your King. Not here.'

'You can't—'

'That's a command,' he snapped. 'When we're alone I'm not your King, and you're not my subject. You're my equal. You may always speak freely—even when I don't like what you're saying.'

'You're *commanding* me to speak freely?' she teased.

'Yes.' He glared at her. 'I want to understand what you're thinking.'

'I already speak my mind—you know you can't stop me. And you already know what I'm thinking. You know you confuse me.'

'Then let me make it simple. All I want, right this second, is to kiss you,' he said plainly. 'Are you willing to let me do that?'

The desire—so new, so rare, promising so much—was irresistible. How could she not explore this—just once—now she finally felt it? It would doubtless be a mistake, but only a little one. And it was one that might be worth the price she would have to pay.

'One kiss,' she breathed. *'One.'*

With slow deliberation he brought his hands to her face and gently tilted her head towards him. She caught the light that kindled in his green gaze as he angled and lowered his head so he could brush his lips against hers in the softest, gentlest sweep.

That wasn't fair. That wasn't a real kiss. And suddenly she realised that she wanted a real kiss—one like that passionate encounter of the other night.

And then he was back, his mouth roving over hers and his tongue teasing her sensitive lips apart. She gasped and he was there, and all that giddy warmth flooded her. She closed her eyes and for the first time truly sank into it. He was so powerful. So commanding. And as he took his time and his care something shifted within her. Then shifted again.

Then he slowly eased the pressure, until he finally lifted his lips but kept his hands framing her face. She kept her eyes firmly closed.

'Was it so awful?' he prompted softly.

She didn't want to look at him and admit the truth. She didn't want to break the magic. She didn't want to go back, or go forward in time, she just wanted to remain suspended in this moment of utter bliss.

'Have I kissed you into a catatonic state?'

She laughed, an irrepressible bubble of delight bursting within her even as tears stung. She blinked them back, opening her eyes to see him—too close, too tender.

'Oh, she breathes, she smiles. She lives.' He was smiling at her, but there was that glint in his eyes. 'Was it so terrible?'

She realised that under that arrogantly teasing question there was concern. Slowly she shook her head. 'Why did you stop? You know you could have done…more.'

'Because I wanted you to *want* more,' he answered with an arrogant shrug. 'I wanted to leave you wanting.'

His honesty was both shocking and thrilling. 'Well that's not fair.'

'Actually, it is. You've left *me* wanting for days now.'

'Unintentionally,' she said indignantly. 'I wasn't even aware.'

'You *were* aware.'

She looked down. She had been aware of the electricity between them. She just hadn't been certain he felt it to the same degree as her. And she hadn't known how to handle it.

She heard him give a muffled groan beneath his breath and he bent closer again.

'I'm going to kiss you again, Kassie. And I'm going to touch you.'

Heat flooded her. 'Where are you going to touch me?'

His smile flashed—wicked and approving—and it made her want to wriggle closer.

'I'm going to kiss you. I'm going to cup and stroke your breasts until they're tight and aching. And then I am going to slide my hand into your panties and touch you where you're hottest. Where you're already wet.'

Her jaw dropped. She was shocked at his explicitness.

'Just my words make you wet.' He took advantage of her parted mouth and kissed her again. Hot and fierce. 'Just my words make you want it.'

She trembled and knew he felt it.

'I think your body knows what it wants,' he muttered. 'I think it knows just what to do.' He pulled her so she was lifted into his lap. 'Are you going to let it?' He kissed her throat. 'Are you going to let *me*?'

Oh, there was no choice at all any more.

'Kiss me…' she breathed.

He didn't hesitate—delivering the long, slow kisses that served to torment her. She wrapped her arms around his neck, holding him close. Never had she known kissing could be so good. So different. So playful. So intense.

He nibbled her lips with a tug of his teeth and then licked the small sting, caressing it with his lips. His hands held her close as he teased her, playfully alternating between soft and shallow kisses and deep lush sweeps of his tongue right inside her mouth. Dizzying, drugging…*delightful.*

Her blood ran hot and hotter still, and she began to wonder if he'd meant what he'd said—if he was ever going to do what he'd promised: touch as well as kiss. She ached for him to go lower, to touch where he'd threatened so wickedly. She was tight and aching all over—not just her breasts but in that hot, secret part of herself.

She moaned—unable to verbalise it. She didn't want to fight it any more, nor to wait. She wanted him to make this ache end.

Slowly, with infinite patience, he kissed down the column of her neck, nipping at the sensitive skin. As he went he gently slid his hand beneath the hem of her tee shirt and up to cup her breast. She gasped as his thumb stroked across the taut tip of her nipple.

'Giorgos…' she moaned.

He returned to kiss her mouth—the gentle teasing replaced with a fierce passion that she instinctively met. An innate urge drove her to suck on his tongue as he plunged it deep into her mouth. His groan of response only made her hungrier.

Readier.

His hand swept down across her stomach firmly. *Finally.* And she was on fire. She moaned again and writhed—twisting to try to get his touch where she wanted it. But he was strong, holding her still while he kissed her and stroked lower, and lower still, slipping his hand beneath the waist of her jeans, beneath the cotton of her panties.

In reflex she pressed her legs together, but all that did was trap his hand—*there*. Right there. His fingers teased. Skilful, knowing fingers. She squirmed as she fought to accept the overwhelming pleasure of his intimate touch.

And acceptance—indeed the need for more—won. Her legs parted and she recklessly pushed her throbbing source of desire against his hand. Because it felt so good. *He* felt so, so good.

And he answered—giving her more, and then more still. That primal pulse thrummed between them. Her hips circled as he drew breathless moans from her until she arched, taut, every muscle screaming with tension as he held her suspended in that long moment of searing, aching need.

She convulsed as pleasure shattered her. Her cry was caught in his rapacious, hard kiss until he released her mouth, allowing her to gasp as she rode the waves he'd summoned within her. In a half delirium she glimpsed him gazing down at her with glittering satisfaction as she came apart in his arms.

She buried her face in his chest so she wouldn't have to meet his searching gaze and he let her, as if he knew she was feeling too exposed, too vulnerable. His fingers stroked through her hair, holding her close, and she could feel the fast beat of his heart and the rapid rise and fall of his chest as he cradled her.

A slow spread of sweetness relaxed every cell, and then more than sweetness…euphoria. It was a joy so sharp she couldn't contain it. She lifted her chin and smiled at him, even as her eyes welled with gratitude, and she felt the fizzing feeling of total goodness.

'That was amazing,' she whispered with unrestrained astonishment. 'Just…amazing. I never… *Gosh.*' She couldn't think of the words to express it.

'That was your first orgasm?'

Something flickered in his eyes as she nodded.

'Thank you.' She pointed her toes as another last spasm of delight rippled through her and puffed out a breath of amazement.

'The pleasure was mine,' he said gruffly. He

stood, tossing her a little in his arms to hold her more easily. 'It's late, Kassie. It's been a big day.'

And it wasn't over yet.

Desire and anticipation hummed throughout her body as he carried her down the corridor to her room and placed her on that big white bed. She sat up, biting her sensitive lip as she wondered what he'd do now. She wanted him to stay close to her and do that again. All caution had burned away in the heat of her attraction to him.

But he pushed her back down on the mattress and then stepped back. 'This time I think we really do need to walk away. I'm not ordering you. I'm asking you.'

'Giorgos…' she breathed.

He shook his head and backed away quickly. 'Have mercy on me.'

Her heart lurched as he closed the door, leaving her alone in that beautiful bedroom. And she finally understood just what a wicked devil he was. He'd done exactly what he'd set out to do. He'd left her wanting.

More.

CHAPTER FIVE

KASSIE WOKE IN a rush, instinctively realising she'd slept late. Given the events of last night, the fact she'd had such a deep, dreamless sleep was incredible. But the big bed was decadently comfortable and the room temperature had been deliciously cool on her hot skin.

She quickly showered and dressed, adrenalin rippling through her veins as she darted along the labyrinthine corridor to his 'lair'. She guessed he'd be there, at work already.

He was sitting at the large table, rather than on the sofa, clad in another of his suits. His frown didn't lighten in the least as he glanced up from his open laptop to watch her walk into the room.

She closed the door and avoided looking at him by focusing on the papers in front of him. One sheet held an incredibly long list of engagements—dates, places, times, people who would be in attendance—but it was the newspapers next to it that claimed her attention.

Kassie's thudding heart sank as she read the bold headlines. The media had gone after Giorgos in their coverage of the astounding news.

King Denied Romance!
Forced into Unhappy Engagement!
True love wins!

The photos they'd included of Giorgos were not kind—his expression was stern in every one—while each picture of Eleni showed her smiling and beautiful. In one she was looking up at her brother as if he were chiding her, but even Kassie understood now that he'd only wanted to do what was best.

'Poor Eleni, bullied by her big brother.' Giorgos's smile didn't reach his eyes. 'Big, bad me.'

'Oh, I don't know.' Kassie smiled. 'It might be nice to have a protective brother…'

She almost wished she'd had one, to stand alongside her and stare down the jerks who'd harassed her.

She glanced at him. 'Why have you gone all frowny face again?'

He was glaring at her. 'I've already told you there is nothing brotherly about what I've done for you. Nor is there anything *nice*.'

He rose from the table and moved around to stand in front of her. That was all he did—just stood that little bit too close, studying her far too intensely with those gleaming eyes. And she reacted—aching for him to take those few inches closer to her.

'Not brotherly,' she choked. 'I got that already.'

He fascinated her, and right now the shadows beneath his eyes were all too human, revealing hurt and worry. Had he got any sleep?

In embarrassment she realised far, *far* too late that while she'd had that 'release', *he* hadn't. She'd gone to bed like the cat who'd got the cream and promptly fallen asleep, while he'd… He'd *what*?

She cringed as she realised she didn't even know if he'd been aroused by what had happened. He'd made it all about *her*—her acquiescence, her pleasure—and taken nothing himself. He'd put her ahead of him. Just as he'd put Eleni ahead of himself now.

'You've taken the blame instead of her,' she said quietly. 'Pinned yourself as the villain to protect her.'

'The speculation will die down quickest that way,' he said dismissively.

'Eventually,' she acknowledged. 'But the commentary isn't kind to you.'

He was being slammed in the press in a way he'd never been slammed before.

'I can handle it.'

He shouldn't have to. He'd only been trying to support his sister.

She skimmed the first paragraphs of the report. 'So they're saying you blocked her romance and that you don't approve of her marriage.'

'And they're be right.'

'You don't *really* think that. I know you want her to be happy.'

'Suddenly you think so much better of me?' A smile quirked the corner of his mouth. 'I'm thinking you must have slept peacefully last night.'

'You'd never have let the marriage go ahead if you hadn't decided to trust her.' Kassie ignored his reference. He'd impressed her and, yes, that was quite a change from only a day ago. But it wasn't because of the way he'd kissed her last night.

'It was in the best interests of the country to get Eleni's situation sorted quickly.' He walked back behind the table.

'It was in *her* best interests. *She* was your priority. Don't deny that.'

'She's *always* been my first priority,' he said dryly. 'You just chose not to see it. But now it seems I'm not quite the monster you first thought.'

He frowned as he turned his laptop to face her. A news service was streaming on the screen.

'It's not just me they've latched on to. They're still outside your apartment. And they've interviewed one of your co-workers. One who met Damon when he visited you. They put you and the hospital as the link between them.'

'Just as you did.' She shrugged.

She chose not to care what they thought of her. She'd heard it all when she was growing up.

'But it wasn't your fault.' He turned to stare at the laptop screen again. 'It was Eleni.' He rubbed his hand over his forehead. 'Nevertheless, it is better for them to think worse of me than her.'

'You think they'd judge her if they knew the truth?'

'Of course they would—you know that.'

'There shouldn't be anything wrong with a woman acting on her desires.'

He suddenly laughed. 'Says *you*, the expert.'

She quietened, embarrassed and a bit hurt. He had no idea…

His expression turned regretful, and then surprisingly tender. 'But it's not like you don't have any desires, is it, Kassie?'

She looked away from him. 'Foolish ones. Ones that shouldn't be acted on.'

'Because you don't want to be judged?' He angled his head so he could keep looking into her eyes. 'The way your mother was judged?'

'I've already been judged. I was judged for years simply for being her daughter—the illegitimate child of the other woman,' she said scornfully. 'That fact made me an instant sex object in my home village when I was a teen and developed curves.' Her gaze narrowed. 'And boys and men don't like it if you say no to them when they've cast you as the village floozy. Then they judge more. And then your reputation is sealed.'

He frowned. 'Did no one defend you?'

'Who *was* there?'

Her mother had kept to herself. Her schoolfriends had become jealous of the attention she attracted. She'd become isolated. And then her mother had got sick and she'd retreated completely.

'That must have been tough on you,' Giorgos said grimly.

'It wasn't so bad. I survived. And I no longer care

what anyone says or thinks of me.' She shrugged off his sympathy because she was stronger for her experience. 'I just want to live my life the way *I* want to.'

'That would be fair enough if you actually did. But you don't. You don't let yourself have that element to your life at all. And you're right—a woman shouldn't be judged at all differently from a man for having sexual desire.'

He glanced again at the screen.

'You shouldn't watch it,' she said, because she did know how it hurt, even when you told yourself not to care.

'I need to know what they're saying so I can figure out my response.'

'What's your usual response?'

'To say nothing. We never comment on personal issues within the royal family.'

'Have there been many?'

'Not in recent years,' he growled.

'So why watch it if you're not going to say anything?' She smiled and shook her head. 'Why let yourself care at all? It isn't worth it.'

'Because I am the King and I am in the public realm. I have a responsibility to my people. What they think is of vital importance.'

'But you're still *human*. Not perfect. You're allowed to make mistakes.'

'I don't want them hurting Eleni,' he said softly.

Kassie looked at the screen. Incessant questions and negative commentary blared from it. 'Perhaps you can show your support for her *and* shut your haters down.'

'How do I do that?' He arched a sceptical eyebrow.

'Why not prove to the world that you're happy to welcome Damon into the family by inviting his parents to dine with you? Show that you're trying to make amends and accept the situation. Open up a bit.'

'Open…? Invite his *parents*?' Giorgos laughed harshly. 'You *know* he's not close to them.'

'That doesn't matter—no one else knows that. They'll come. They love nothing more than sucking up to powerful people,' she said bitterly.

He looked at the screen through narrowed eyes and then looked at her. 'Perhaps I don't need to invite his parents,' he said slowly. 'Not when I already have *you* right here.'

'I'm the *scandal* of the family.' She recoiled. 'You can't use *me* to regain your approval ratings.'

'Actually, that's all the more reason to use you,'

he mused thoughtfully. 'If I'm willing to accept his illegitimate half-sister, then I'm showing just how open-minded and progressive my monarchy is becoming.'

For a moment she was thrilled at the thought of him accepting her publicly—of him spending time with her as if he were proud to. Her pulse quickened. 'Are you going to let me drag you into the modern world, King Giorgos?'

He kept studying her, an odd light in his eye. But then he sighed. 'I'm not. No.'

Disappointment hit and it was strong. 'Why not?'

'What was the point of my bringing you here to escape the press hounds if I now set you right amongst them?' He walked over to put his hands on her shoulders and smiled at her. 'But it wasn't a bad idea.'

'*Must* you be so patronising?' she grumbled. 'It's obviously a fantastic idea. You can control media access to me. Isn't that what you've always done anyway, for both you and Eleni?'

The more she thought about it, the better it seemed. She could help him. And she wanted to.

'I won't let you down. Believe it or not, I *can* stay silent when I need to.'

'Believe it or not, I don't *want* you to stay silent.' He drew her close.

'Giorgos...be serious.' She couldn't hold back her smile at him. 'I can *help* you here.'

'Do I need help?'

'Perhaps it's okay to protect yourself as much as it is to protect your sister. And to protect your sister's husband's half-sister—who is in no way any kind of sister to *you*.'

His sudden amusement was good to see and her pulse skipped.

But then he sobered. 'You don't want people to judge you,' he said. 'I cannot put you in such a public position. I won't use you like that.'

'You haven't been listening to me,' she muttered. 'I don't give a damn what they say about me. You're the only one who cares about that. And, let's face it, the media are already on me—literally digging in my garbage, for goodness' sake. All because I'm Damon's distant relative. Hiding from them isn't going to work long-term. But you presenting me to them might assuage that initial interest. And they won't give a damn about me once they discover how boring I am. I can take advantage of your authority over the media.'

He regarded her closely, clearly thinking hard

but revealing little. 'Why would you want to do this for me?'

He shook her gently, but she felt the tension in his body as he angled closer to her, as if he couldn't help himself.

She lowered her lashes demurely. 'You're my King.'

She heard his sharp intake of breath.

'Is there nothing you want from me in return?' he asked silkily, bending closer. 'No way in which I can help you?'

Oh, he was a devil. His words invoked a temptation within her and the possibilities of this situation swiftly crystallised—clearly. She wanted to feel what she'd felt with him before. She could take advantage of his obvious expertise in that area too. Just *once*. Just for herself.

'Maybe I'll stay here for a few more days,' she said breathlessly. 'I'll be seen with you, just as a distant family member, to show your acceptance of Eleni's marriage.' Her heart pounded.

'And in return…' He watched her solemnly, looking every bit the powerful plunderer. 'How may I help you, Ms Marron?'

He only called her that when he was feeling edgy…when he was exerting inner control.

'You know already,' she said, very low.

'You want me.'

'Yes.' She swallowed and pushed through her nerves. 'Teach me. Everything. I know there's nothing afterwards. I don't want any claim on you. Or any relationship. I just want the moment. Now.'

'Why?'

'Why do you think?' She tossed her head and glared up at him, angry with him for making her confess *everything*. 'I've never wanted this with anyone before. I thought I wasn't…*normal*. I want to be normal. Perhaps if I've done it once and liked it then I can like it again…with someone else.'

He suddenly stilled. 'Done what once? I only helped you to orgasm last night.'

'I'm not talking about orgasms.'

His jaw dropped. 'Are you telling me you've never done this…at *all*?'

'I'm a virgin, Giorgos.' She was suddenly burning.

'How…?' he breathed.

'What do you mean, how?'

'You're twenty-three. You're…'

'What?'

His gaze skittered across her body and he hesitated a second. 'Beautiful.'

'You mean buxom. But, you know, the size of my erogenous zones doesn't equate with their ability to actually work.' She felt herself blushing all over. 'I already told you—I don't like to be touched. At least I didn't,' she corrected with a mumble. 'But I liked what *you* did.'

And she wanted to know that she could get everything within her working properly. He could help her with that.

He released her shoulders and stepped back, shoving his hands into his pockets.

'My virginity doesn't matter,' she added quickly, when she saw his expression shut down as he turned away. 'It's just circumstance. Don't make it into something it isn't.'

He whirled back to face her. 'How can you say it doesn't matter?'

'Did *your* first time matter?' She blushed furiously as she asked.

He huffed out a harsh breath. 'My first time was with a woman who was a little older than me and a whole lot more experienced.'

Despite herself, she was diverted. 'How old *were* you?'

A rueful smile quirked his lips. 'You don't want to know. It was scandalous.'

'Oh, I want to know,' she muttered. 'You can't shock me.'

'I think I can,' he laughed. 'I was fifteen—she was twenty-six.'

Kassie didn't know whether to be awed or appalled. 'Were you in love with her?'

'I was incredibly grateful. She was a generous teacher.'

Jealousy smarted. 'You were with her for a while?'

He looked somewhat uncomfortable. 'I was young, brash and hungry. I was with many young women in my late teens.'

Kassie's eyes widened in surprise. 'You were a man whore?'

'I...' He looked startled, but then laughed. 'I guess you could say that.'

'But you never have a girlfriend.'

She frowned. There'd never been a whisper of romance regarding the King in the press. According to the media he just worked hard all the time. But was he still a secret man whore? Well, *duh*. Given his skill, of course he must be. But how could he have a string of lovers and no one know anything about it?

'Occasionally I do. Discreetly.'

'Discreetly?' She stared at him with blatant disbelief. 'You can't help but tease me that way… Every other utterance between us is inappropriate.'

He suddenly laughed. 'Only with you. And only because it bothers you so much.'

So he didn't flirt shamelessly with every woman he met? An odd twinge of relief softened her. 'Do they last long? Do you care for them?'

Could she be one of his girlfriends for just a little while?

'I trust them as far as I'm able to trust anyone.'

She swallowed hard. 'In my experience, that's not very far.' And trust was a different thing from *caring*.

But he didn't reply.

'Why is that?' she prompted him. 'What woman betrayed you?'

He was Europe's most eligible bachelor, but he wasn't known as any kind of 'Playboy Prince'. He was too hardworking, too serious.

'There's no way I can casually date, or meet someone new without the world watching. And

I think it takes time and space to build trust,' he said, failing to answer her actual question.

Well, that was fair enough, but he wasn't exactly trying with anyone, was he? And then she understood why. He was all about duty.

'Caring doesn't matter, does it?' she realised. 'Because you'll settle for some sort of arranged marriage with a princess of some remote European country some time.'

He paused and looked her directly in the eyes. 'Yes.'

She was quiet, processing this flat acceptance of a future so unloving.

He kept looking into her eyes, and suddenly intensity stormed into him. 'Won't it make it awkward in the future if we have an affair now?'

Was he going to agree to her terms?

She tried to suck in some much-needed oxygen. 'Awkward in what way?'

'At family events?'

'*What* family events?' She suddenly giggled. 'I'm barely *family*. I'm not going to come to the palace for Christmas.'

'What *do* you do for Christmas?' He cocked his head.

'I work on the ward.'

'Of course you do.'

'I'm not an angel.'

'No?'

'Of course not. I'm as human as you are.'

'But we both know I'm better than most,' he teased. 'Why else would you be asking me to teach you the delights of carnal desire?'

'Don't tease.'

'Then tell me *why*,' he suddenly snapped. 'Honestly. How do you think this can possibly work? How, in any way, do you not get hurt in this?'

Oh, so he assumed that *she'd* get hurt but not him?

'I know you're not going to hurt me because you *can't* hurt me,' she answered vehemently. 'This is just for now—while I'm staying. Then it ends. You can't keep me strung along for months or years because no one can know. It can't even last weeks because of the risk of being found out—I know that's a risk you won't take. You can't marry me. You can't love me. You're no threat to me long-term. I'm safe from hurt simply because of the truth of our circumstances.'

She already knew this would lead nowhere—other than to a hopefully awesome experience for herself. One she really didn't want to miss out on. Not now she'd had a *glimpse*.

'And you're not going to fall in love with me?'

She refused to rise to his arrogant baiting. 'I'm not going to be with you long enough for that to be possible.'

'You think falling in love is dependent on time? Is there no such thing as love at first sight?'

'Of course not,' she snapped. 'Lust, yes. Love? That takes longer to develop. You just said yourself—it takes time to build trust and caring and all that stuff.'

'I'm *so* glad you're such an expert on this. You've satisfactorily allayed *all* my concerns.'

She flushed. 'Don't be facetious.'

She wasn't going to fall for him. She just wanted to be 'cured'—to feel normal sexual arousal, to have sex. *Good* sex. If she could do it with him, then she could do it with someone else in the future…

But her innards curled with distaste at that thought. And there was the truth: she couldn't regret this happening because if she didn't get that with any other guy then she would at least have experienced it once with *him*. She wouldn't have missed out on that sensation in her life. Because up till now, she'd been sure she would never feel it.

'Don't tell me you didn't try to tempt me into this,' she said softly. 'Don't act like this isn't exactly what you want.' The colour flamed in her cheeks as she called him on it.

If he denied her, when she'd felt his passion, she'd be angry. She wanted to be able to trust her instincts as she discovered her sensuality.

'Okay. I won't lie. I want you. Our chemistry is off the charts. Maybe it's because it's so damn inappropriate. Mostly it's because you're so bloody beautiful and you set my teeth on edge every time you open your mouth. And, yes, I wanted you to come to me like this. I wanted to provoke you.'

A wave of satisfaction swept over her. 'Then what are you waiting for?'

He stared at her for a second and his eyes widened. 'You think I'm going to tumble you into bed this second?'

'Why not?'

Hadn't she waited all her life already? She'd never wanted a man like this. She'd always run from any possible encounter. Every barrier she could raise, she'd erected. But now? This was her one chance to be normal. To feel again what she'd felt last night.

He laughed delightedly, but then groaned. 'Kassie, you're enough to tempt a man into total madness.'

'Don't laugh at me.'

'I'm not laughing *at* you.' He cupped her face and looked into her eyes. 'All your life you've missed out on the build-up, the anticipation.'

'I don't need to anticipate this any more than I already do.' He didn't get it. 'This is a first for me. I want it to become *normal* for me, the way it is for everyone else.'

He dragged in a breath. 'If you trust me to do this, then trust me enough to do it my way.'

She paused, a curl of anticipation flickering through her. 'Are you being bossy again?'

He lifted a shoulder. 'What did you expect? Leopards can't change their spots, and I've been the boss almost all my life. Give me some leeway. I won't let you down.' He sighed. 'And the very least you can do is have some breakfast. You must be hungry…' His eyes lit with laughter. 'For *food*. Come on.'

He led her out into a small private patio. Her

mouth watered as she saw a silver tray laden with pastries and fruit.

'Let's start with this, okay?' he said.

'With what?'

He lifted a finger. 'Touch your finger to mine.'

She pressed the tip of her finger lightly against his.

'Look at me.'

How was it possible for her to sizzle with just this tiny, most innocuous of touches? But it wasn't tiny, and somehow she couldn't tear her gaze from his. The connection, just from touching fingertip to fingertip and looking right into his eyes, was insanely strong.

Desire shook like a quake deep within her. She shivered with longing. 'This is—'

'Intimate,' he said softly. 'This is going to be *very* intimate, Kassie, don't try to tell yourself it isn't.'

She had to resist the sudden urge to pull back.

He saw it and he smiled. 'That's why we're going to take our time and start with the simple sweetness of holding hands.'

Warmth bloomed as his fingers laced through hers.

'I'm not twelve,' she grumbled beneath her breath, and grabbed a pastry with her free hand.

'Thank heavens for that.' He laughed. 'You know to ask for anything you'd like to eat? Swim. Read anything you can find in the library.' He glanced at his watch and frowned. 'Now I have to go—I can't be late to my meeting.' He looked at their entwined hands and then released her. 'We'll have dinner out here tonight.'

'You don't need to romance me. I've already said yes. In fact, I'm the one who asked.'

'I don't need to *romance* you…?' His shoulders shook. 'You just want wham, bam and it's all over?'

'I've never felt desire like normal people—' She broke off and glared at him. 'Why are you laughing *again*?'

'What makes you think this level of desire is *normal*?'

She didn't want to think this was anything more or less than normal. 'This isn't anything special.'

He looked at her seriously. 'One thing I learned from my debauched youth is that perhaps it *should* be special. Especially the first time.'

She shook her head.

'In this moment, Kassie,' he explained with seemingly infinite patience. 'I'm not talking for ever. I'm talking in this moment. We let this be special in this moment. Okay?'

'At least I know you're not going to kiss and tell,' she said with a wry smile. 'I know I can trust you to keep this discreet.'

Giorgos requested his driver go slow, so he could prepare properly for his meeting, but he couldn't get his mind off Kassie. He'd trusted no woman this way in years, never bringing one into his home. He relied on clandestine rendezvous in the private house he kept in the city for that express purpose.

He had no desire to take Kassie there. But Kassie wasn't like other women. Kassie was just… Kassie. And she looked at him with such innocently questioning hunger that he nearly lost his head completely. Rationally, he knew he shouldn't touch her. He should send her away. He could keep her safe far away from his side. But he couldn't resist keeping her close. He was tired of the guilt and obligation he would have for the rest of his life. He wanted to feel better. Helping Kassie made him feel better.

Liar.

He grimaced. She made him feel like a god.

Or, more accurately, a selfish, greedy devil. He wanted more than he deserved. But couldn't he have it just this once? For over a decade now he'd been the perfectly behaved Prince, dutifully fulfilling his destiny, maintaining everything as it ought to be maintained… He'd not set a foot across the line of being discreet and controlled.

Until Kassie. Within two minutes of meeting her he'd crossed the line to inappropriate and then full-on outrageous. But it went both ways. Whatever chemistry was between them, it was strong. He shouldn't have agreed to her request, but it felt right to get rid of the attraction between them. And the only way to do that was by sleeping together. Ignoring it would only make it worsen and he'd always wonder *what if?*

He had enough regrets to live with already. And he truly did want to help her—she thought she was damaged, that she wasn't normal, and she wanted to feel things. He wanted that for her too—he wanted nothing more than to see her flushed and screaming with pleasure. And sated. Her honesty and her courage in what she'd asked had floored him.

He tried again to focus on the meeting preparation. He had wanted to prove he could resist his desperate urge to tumble her into bed there and then. Hell, he'd wanted to. But he had to be able to take it or leave it as he chose. And, more importantly, he needed to give her the space and time to change her mind.

If she didn't, then they'd have their moment. He'd take her slowly and savour every second, make sure she was right there with him every step of the way. He was determined to make it the best for her. He almost couldn't cope with the prospect of burying himself deep in her lush, tight body—of showing her just what she was built for. His mouth dried and his muscles bunched.

Ignoring the meeting notes, he sent a message to his secretary, requesting dressing assistance for Kassie—because the bargain had been struck and she'd want to maintain her end of the deal. She had pride—he understood that about her. And he respected her for it.

He didn't return until nightfall, semi-pleased with the way his day had gone—with his ability to concentrate on the meeting. He *could* keep everything under control with Kassie.

But within two minutes of him getting back to the house trouble hit. She was there. She was beautiful. And she had that teasing, disarming smile on her face as she looked up from where she lounged on his sofa. The sofa where he'd made her scream her release last night.

'How'd it go?' she asked.

For a moment Giorgos didn't know what she meant as she looked at him with warmth and expectation in her gorgeous eyes. Was she asking him about his meeting?

'Fine,' he answered awkwardly.

'They didn't give you a hard time?'

She really wanted to know. No one *ever* asked him how his day had gone. Because usually no one was waiting for him to return home. His sister had always been at the classes he'd arranged for her, and his assistants had been busy fulfilling his requests. He'd always turned his focus to the next meeting, the next event, the next decision.

He rubbed his hair as he realised she was still sitting there, waiting for a reply, her eyebrows slowly lifting.

'A hard time?' He shook his head. 'Not to my face. They wouldn't dare.' He sighed. 'Most of those at the meeting today know to hold their tongue.'

No one had ever loitered, waiting for him to return, to ask him how his day had gone. That

Kassie was dong so now touched him. He grimaced at his newfound neediness. If he told her that he liked it she'd probably call him out for being sexist or something—expecting to have a woman waiting for him at home. Truth was he didn't ever expect to have that. He couldn't ask someone for that. But all the same it was nice… just this once.

'Because they're afraid of you?' she asked.

'I hope not. I think they just know it's pointless. We have work to be getting on with, we can't be wasting time on…that stuff.'

'So you just keep going with the "to do" list?'

'Because the "to do" list is important.'

'So is taking a break—you told me that yourself. Maybe this is a good time to take a break.'

He rather liked the contrary mix of subtle ribbing underpinned by gentle concern. It could be reciprocated.

'How was *your* day?' he asked, but he had to cough away the huskiness. Was he *this* unused to enquiring after someone? How socially inept *was* he in this level of simple intimacy?

'It was good.' Her smile was shy.

Well, that wasn't enough of an answer. 'What did you do?'

'I went for a swim. I raided your library. I watched a movie.' She listed them all off.

It still wasn't enough. He wanted to know whether she'd truly had a nice afternoon. He wished he'd been here to see for himself.

'A movie?' He sat on the sofa arm and tugged off his tie. 'What movies do you like?'

'Action.'

He glanced at her keenly. There'd been a distinct sensual purr to that reply. 'And now you want action of your own?'

'Don't you think you've kept me waiting long enough?' She leaned closer with a confidential whisper, even as that blush swept across her beautiful face. 'I'm ready to progress from the holding hands phase.'

He took her hand in his and felt the jolt of electricity. His entire body stiffened in anticipation. 'Are you, now? What if I'm not?'

'You're the experienced one here—why do you need to prolong this? We don't have all that much time.'

'And you want to make the most of it?'

'Do you blame me?'

She was going to kill him. She was so sweet, so eager, and so damn inexperienced. He released her hand to slide off the elastic tie securing her braid and slowly began to release the sleek twists of her hair.

'Well, then, I should prepare you. We're not going all the way tonight, Kassie.'

Her pout appeared. 'Why not?'

Because that was what he'd decided. For her benefit and to prove his own self-control.

'There are other things to take pleasure in first.' He skimmed his hands down her arms.

Those bewitching deep brown eyes widened farther still, until they dominated her beautiful face.

His gut tightened. 'Let me show you what I mean.'

He'd been longing to do this for days. To kiss every inch of her soft body. If she could put herself entirely into his hands now, then they'd find the ultimate pleasure when he finally claimed her completely.

He tried to take his time, to savour his first full taste of her, knowing that this was her initiation into this deliciously intimate delight. He tried to stay gentle. But the scent and sweet warmth of her, the unguarded, untutored response of her, made it impossible. As he finally peeled her panties to the side he glanced up, catching wariness and embarrassment, but also determination. And trust.

He vowed again, deep within himself, to help her conquer the instinctive resistance that she sought to overcome with soft kisses, firm hands and patience.

'I have you, Kassie,' he murmured as she shivered and squirmed beneath his touch. 'I won't hurt you.' He wanted only to bring her pleasure. Suddenly it seemed to be his most important mission in life. 'You can let me do anything.'

The softest sigh escaped her and those slender, long legs parted. He tasted the heated acceptance of her body with its slick welcome for his tongue. He kissed her, sucking softly on that small, sensitive bud. She stiffened and he heard her catch back her cry.

'There's no one to hear you but me,' he muttered hungrily. 'Don't hold anything back.'

And then, to his intense satisfaction, she didn't.

'Kassie,' he said softly. 'Look at me.'

Panting, she obeyed, opening her eyes to look straight into his. That feeling was still spreading though her body, honeyed bliss seeping into every cell. Her smile blossomed and a laugh bubbled out of her. The exquisite feelings of lightness and happiness were uncontainable.

He brushed her hair back from her face and his expression softened. 'Not so bad?'

Little aftershocks ricocheted around her body and she knew he felt them. He was holding her loosely. Carefully. Talking gently and ensuring she was centred. For just this moment—just this once—she fully appreciated the strength of his protectiveness.

'What about you?' She paused, realising he hadn't had the same release she had. He was still aroused and unfulfilled. 'Your…partners…they reciprocate in the same way?'

'I don't expect you to.'

That jarred. She didn't want him treating her as anything less or anything more than his other 'companions'. She sat up, realising that the King was on his knees on the floor in front of her. 'What if I want to?'

Something flickered in his eyes and he slowly shook his head.

'Consider this part of the exploration of *my* needs. I'm curious.' She glanced down his body, still hidden in one of those damned perfect suits. 'I want to understand how this works for you too.'

She wanted to know how he looked, how he felt, in that ultimately vulnerable moment. She didn't want him to hold that back from her. 'It's only fair.'

'You have a fixation with fairness.'

'I want to explore everything about this attraction. *All* senses.' Suddenly she was angry and embarrassed by his denial. 'I don't want you martyring yourself for me,' she said harshly. 'Making this all about my pleasure only—as if you getting me off somehow makes you a better person. Just because you've helped a poor frigid girl get to orgasm. I want you to *want* me. To have me the way you want to. To have the pleasure that I have. The way you want it.'

He stared at her, colour deepening in his face. 'Kassie…'

'I told you already,' she whispered fiercely. 'I haven't got anything to lose here. I want what I want and how I want it. If you don't want me the same way I want you, then walk away. I'm not going to be your charity case.'

He moved so quickly she sucked in a shocked breath. He savagely strained forward, pushing her back against the sofa, grinding his hips against hers.

'Does *this* feel like I don't want you?'

The rigid length of his erection dug into her stomach. Her toes curled. How was it that it took only this? Only a few words and a simple touch for her to be so aroused when she'd never been turned on before in all her life?

She trembled and gripped his hips as he lifted away from her. She wriggled beneath him, sliding lower until she slipped right off the sofa and was sitting on the floor, while he was up on his knees before her. She heard his muffled swearing and tilted her head so she could see up into his face.

'Teach me,' she said simply. 'What do you want me to do? How can I please you?'

'You only have to look at me like that and you're halfway there.' He looked into her eyes. 'Kiss me,' he muttered rapidly. 'Touch me. I ache for you to touch me.'

She fumbled, butter-fingered, with his belt and zipper. Half-laughing, half-cursing, he helped her until his manhood jutted free. Her jaw dropped at the sight of him—the size. She licked her dried lips.

He groaned harshly. 'Just touch me.'

His skin was flushed and she realised how near to the edge he was. And so she touched him. Gently at first, then with greater pressure as she felt him press against her. With one hand, then two. And then with her tongue.

Could she make such a strong and powerful man tremble? Power sluiced through her veins as she gained knowledge of him. She used her mouth, kissing him hard, sucking and stroking, taking him in as deeply as she possibly could.

'Stop, Kassie.' His fingers tightened painfully on her shoulders and he pulled her away. *'Stop.'*

'Why?' she demanded plaintively, desperately wanting to continue. Because that had felt good to her too. That had felt exciting. 'Did I do it wrong?'

'No.' He shook his head, his breath shuddering.

'But you didn't…'

'Not this first time.'

'I'm not scared. I want to—'

'Kassie.' He hauled her up to sit on the sofa, so he could stare into her eyes. 'I know what you want—and you'll have it. But I have wants too. And I don't want my release until I'm tight inside you. I want to lose myself in you. Right inside you.' He rested his forehead on hers. His gaze was close and searching. 'Kassie?'

'Okay.' Kassie's pulse slowly settled and a poignant longing trickled into the lingering warmth.

She wanted that too. She wanted that more than she'd ever wanted anything. 'But why have you stopped?'

'Because I told you before we started that we weren't going all the way tonight. This is enough for now.'

'No, it isn't.' Why on earth would he possibly think that this was *enough*? 'I'm not going to regret this. I want you. I want *this*.'

'Not tonight, Kassie.'

She stood up, a streak of coldness entering her bloodstream. 'You think I'm going to change my mind.'

He too stood, and reached for her wrist, holding her close while keeping her away from him at the same time. 'I'm giving you a chance. One last chance.'

She looked at him seriously. 'I don't need you to protect me in this way.'

'Perhaps I'm protecting myself.'

She shook her head. He wasn't. He was being the King—the decision-maker, the protector. The dominator. But she would forgive him this once, because she wanted what she knew he would give her in the end.

It wasn't easy for him to walk away from her

now. His chest rose and fell rapidly as she stepped away from him. His lips twisted, as if he were regretting her obedience. She wanted to tease him for that, in the same way that he'd teased her. The remnants of that languid feeling made her movements relaxed and assured. Confidence in her body soared. In their chemistry.

She suddenly turned back and strolled towards him. He didn't move as she reached up and kissed him the way she'd learned from him—with all her aggression and desire—until she felt his tension snap and he jerked back from her with an audible gasp. The fire in his eyes should have alarmed her. Instead she sent him a soft smile of pure satisfaction.

'Get to your room,' he ordered huskily. 'And lock the damn door.'

'If I don't?' she murmured back. 'Will you tie me to the bed?'

He stepped after her again, gripping her wrists and twisting her arms to pin them tight behind her back, pushing her body hard into his.

He retaliated just as she'd desired—kissing her with complete carnal dominance until she was breathing hard and begging. But he just stood there, his feet planted wide, his hands exerting such control—holding her fast even as he tormented her, reducing her to nothing more than a mass of need and pleasure just by using his mouth.

'Go to bed, Kassie,' he growled, and released her. He strode to the door, opening it and waiting for her to walk through it. 'Go *now*.'

'Why do you have to be so controlling?' she whispered in reproof as she stalked past him. 'You know I'm no threat to you.'

CHAPTER SIX

SHE WAS AN *absolute* threat. He needed to prove to himself that not all his control was gone. But in the smallest hours he lay wide awake. He was fooling himself. He had *zero* control left—and he was reduced to fantasising about how he'd make it the best for her, imagining all different scenarios and tying himself in knots.

What she'd asked of him was so personal, and it was a privilege that he refused to abuse. While it was a delight for him too, this was about *her*. Perhaps he could even think of it as one little redress in the balance of guilt he carried.

Conceited jerk.

He threw back the sheet and stalked to get a fresh glass of water. As if he were doing *her* a favour! This was all for *him*. He wanted her in every way and he'd manipulated her into being here. Into staying. Into asking him to take her virginity. He'd done everything he could to get her in his grasp. Hell, he'd effectively kidnapped her from the hospital. The 'pause' he'd insisted on tonight was nothing more than a lame attempt to ease his conscience over yet another moment of guilt…

But it was buying her some time to ensure she truly wanted this, right? He figured nothing would make that decision clearer for her than being presented with it in the cold light of day. So he'd suffer through the agony of lust through the long, slow night. That was the least penance he could do.

Kassie woke late again, but she didn't feel as rested; she felt hot and niggly. *Needy.* She wanted to confront him and provoke him into finishing what they'd started last night. She just didn't quite know how. No doubt he'd be working already, anyway, and she'd have to wait through another whole torturous day.

He was high-handed. Arrogant. *Honourable.* Which was utterly annoying. Why did he have to be so protective? Why wouldn't he throw caution to the wind and take this risk? What *was* it that had caused him to have such little trust in people?

Bothered, she got out of bed and picked a strawberry from the breakfast tray that had been delivered to her private lounge. She bit into the fruit and felt her body eagerly absorb the fuel, but those edgy fires still smouldered within her.

She slipped on the simple white bikini she'd borrowed from the collection in the pool room the previous day. It was the only one decent enough to cover her curves. She walked down the cool corridor to the cave that had been incorporated into the building. There she discovered that Giorgos wasn't working. He was swimming lengths in the sheltered end of the crystalline pool. His movements were powerful and strong and, if her eyes weren't deceiving her, he was swimming *naked*.

She leaned back against the wall, her knees absurdly weakened as heat burnished her body. From the tips of her toes to the very top of her head she felt the driving urge to touch.

He slowed, then lifted his head to stare at her.

'You're not working.' She wanted him to swim nearer.

He stayed low in the water. 'I'm trying to keep my cool.'

'Are you angry?'

'Not angry, no.'

'Didn't you sleep well?' she asked innocently.

Intent flashed in his eyes. 'Come into the water with me.'

Anticipation slid over her skin—warm feather strokes that caused shivers. Because no doubt he meant that literally. But she slowly shook her head, because the truth was she didn't think she could actually stand on her own two feet right now.

'Ah…' He swam to the edge of the pool nearest her. 'If the mountain won't go to Mohammed, then Mohammed must go to the mountain.'

'Are you calling me a mountain?'

'A snow-capped, ice-cold, beautiful mountain. One that hides a volcano two hundred feet down. One with a *very* molten core.'

'Oh, please.' She rolled her eyes.

But that core was already melting, and he chose that moment to lever himself out of the pool onto the edge in a single swift movement. As she'd suspected, he was utterly, gloriously naked. What she hadn't realised was that he was aroused. Hugely, undeniably aroused.

Kassie's jaw dropped as she struggled to breathe. She couldn't speak—couldn't tear her gaze from the pulsing vision of complete masculinity. She'd known he was big, but she hadn't factored in that he'd be as big…*everywhere*… Or that his muscles would be so honed, so deeply defined.

His hard erection jutted, straining high. She'd touched him there—kissed him there—last night. An intense need to do that again rocked her. Here. Now. The wave of sheer lust was so fierce she trembled like a flimsy blossom in a storm.

He stood unashamedly watching her reaction with heat and amusement in his eyes. 'Does the sight of me scare you?'

'I don't think "scare" is the right word,' she croaked.

Lazily he picked up a white towel from the folded stack on a nearby table. 'What *is* the right word?'

'Awe,' she mumbled. 'Shock and awe.'

She watched, leaning limply against the wall as he wrapped the towel around himself, hiding him from her view.

'Spoilsport,' she whispered.

He didn't stop fastening the towel, but he stepped closer. 'You slept okay?'

She nodded and swallowed. 'And now we have the entire day before us.'

He cupped her cheek. 'No, we don't.'

At the touch of his fingers on her she felt that heat roll over her again. 'Why not?'

He didn't answer. He was too busy looking at

her mouth. It was almost as if he wasn't aware of anything else any more. Her lashes lowered lazily—her eyes wanting to focus only on him. He was so magnificent.

And then he kissed her. That fire deep within her fizzed, launching those exquisite sensations into every limb—weakening, warming… She was so willing. And he *knew*.

Suddenly his mouth and his hands were everywhere. He pushed aside the cups of her bikini top so he could nuzzle her breasts. The way he worshipped them made fierce pride blossom. Never had she liked her body the way she did today—now she revelled in it. And as he kissed her breasts one hand delved lower still, skimming beneath her bikini bottoms. She liked this too—arching her hips away from the wall to press into his teasing hand.

He sent her a look of satisfaction before claiming her mouth. She liked that even more. And as he plundered her mouth with his tongue, in teasing, deep licks, he parted her intimately, stroking her slick seam before slowly sliding a finger inside. She gasped, tensing, but he kept rubbing back and forth across her sensitive nub with his thumb and she shivered as that delicious, foreign feeling strained her control.

'That's it,' he muttered in between those crushingly passionate kisses as she moaned and began to rock against him. 'You're so hot.'

He worked in and out, sliding faster and faster, deeper. Her hips bucked as she became accustomed to riding him. As she became enraptured. She was so hot, so spellbound by the sensations he stirred, she was almost rendered catatonic as he'd once teased her she would be.

Her eyes closed and she helplessly—brazenly—moaned every time he pressed closer, as the towel around him gently abraded the ultra-sensitive skin of her upper thighs. The pressure of his body was unbearably good. She wanted to slither to the floor and feel all of his weight above her, all of him within her. But it was too late. She was shuddering—screaming—as he shot her to the stars.

'How many times are you going to make me lose control like this before you give me what I want?' she groaned breathlessly, her eyes still closed.

'Dozens,' he admitted, pulling her so she rested against his broad chest. 'Dozens and dozens.' He gently rubbed circles on her back. 'It's something you should enjoy every day. You're getting used to feeling that hot need. You're not resisting the sensations any more—you're embracing them. You're less afraid.'

'I'm not afraid at all.' Not with him.

Her limbs tingled. That rush of pleasure had only made her more determined than ever.

'Then you're nearly ready.'

'I'm ready now.'

'Then the anticipation will make it even better.' He stepped back.

She hadn't realised that she could still feel frustration despite just having had the pleasure of orgasm. She was so close to experiencing it all and she wanted it now.

'But—'

'I have found a suitable event for you to accompany me to,' he interrupted.

'An event?' she muttered, aghast. 'Today?'

How could she *possibly* pull herself together enough to appear in public after that shattering experience?

Amusement warmed his expression. 'A personal grooming assistant is arriving shortly. She'll have a selection of outfits for you and she can style your hair and make-up. You'll get the Cinderella treatment you missed out on.'

Personal grooming? Rebellion rose. She hadn't meant it when she'd said she wanted a new wardrobe—she'd just wanted to disagree with him. And, from the teasing gleam in his eye now, he knew it.

'Of course you *could* wear your hospital uniform, or those worn jeans you had on yesterday.' He shrugged. 'But the world will be judging. There'll be an article in the press analysing every item you're wearing with designer and price details attached.'

'They won't be interested in what I'm wearing. I'm only Damon's half-sister.'

'They're interested in any woman within five feet of my vicinity,' he said, displaying his innate supreme arrogance.

She rolled her eyes. 'Because really they're mostly interested in you?'

'Truthfully? I think you'll find there is a strong fascination with you.'

She frowned and shook her head, but he cupped her cheek, stilling her.

'It's human nature to admire uncommonly beautiful things, Kassie. We can't help ourselves. You know you draw attention from both men and women, young and old alike. It doesn't matter whether you're wearing a sack or a G-string—they're still going to stare.'

He thought she was uncommonly beautiful? A tiny spark glowed inside her—because from him that was nice. But *only* from him. Not from the rest of the world.

'They'll see me as a sex object,' she muttered. 'Because of my shape.' They'd done that to her mother.

'Everyone does that to you initially, don't they?' he muttered. 'That's why you work so hard to prove that there's more to you. Even when you shouldn't have to prove it. Even when they should just know.'

His astuteness surprised and pleased her—but then she realised he understood because he was the same.

'You do that too,' she said slowly. 'You work hard to prove yourself as King. All the time.'

But when he was alone, unhindered by all the world watching him, there was another element visible to her. He had something caged within him that he wouldn't let the rest of the world see.

'I have far more to prove—for far more nefarious reasons than being good-looking.' He waggled his brows at hers.

'*Ridiculously* good-looking,' she amended with a gurgling laugh as she realised that something of what he kept locked away in public was his sense of humour.

'They see me as a sex object because of my birth—my title, money, power.'

'They'd see you as a sex object *without* the title, money or power,' she corrected him dryly. 'It's your face and your physique. Muscles cause brain meltdowns, you understand.'

'Because we can't help but admire beautiful things,' he reiterated with a chuckle. 'I ignore it. You can ignore it too.'

'Yet you want me to dress up for them?'

'I want you to be comfortable. That doesn't have to mean a designer dress and layers of make-up if you don't want it to. Do what you wish,' he said dismissively.

For half a moment she felt like wearing something completely outrageous—just to shock him and the rest of the world.

'In the end it makes no difference to me,' he added wickedly. 'You'll still end up naked in my bed tonight.'

She stared at him—stunned. 'It makes a *huge* difference to you. You're *all* about appearances. You're the one who cares about that too much—not me.'

'You think?'

'I *know*. Everything is just so. Everything is perfect and proper and done the way it's been done for decades.'

'Not everything is proper. And everything is definitely *not* perfect.'

'No?' She dared him to explain. 'What *is* it you think you have to prove? What *are* those nefarious reasons?'

That roguish glint in his eyes sparked. 'Too terrible to talk about.'

'I don't believe you,' she said softly.

'Why not?' His amusement faded. 'When have I lied to you?'

She waited him out.

'Too terrible,' he repeated quietly, with no teasing in his eyes at all now. 'Don't ask again.'

'So you're going to leave me hanging just because you want your moment of mystery? You don't need to catch me on a hook and reel me in, or play some kind of obscure pity card. I'm already going to leap into your bed the second you finally crook your little finger.'

She shocked a low laugh out of him. 'You're saying I can *trust* you?'

'Why would you think you couldn't?' She was stupidly wounded by his laugh. 'I'm going to let you inside me.'

'I don't trust *anyone*,' he said quietly. 'Don't take it personally. I didn't even trust my own sister's judgement. Now she's left with Damon. I've pushed her away.'

'No, you haven't. She knows you love her. And she loves *you*—that's why she was worried about letting you down. You've proved you're trying to trust her now by letting her go,' she said softly. 'So why can't you try with me too?'

'That isn't what it is between us.'

'So it's okay for you to help *me* with something, but you won't let me do the same for you?'

'What makes you think *you* can help?'

She flinched as his riposte dumped her right back into *her place*. Who did she think she was? 'Of course. Silly me. I can't.'

'Kassie.' He sighed. 'Doing this with you is a sign of trust for me. But just because we're physically intimate it doesn't mean I have to open up all my past agonies to you.'

So there *were* past agonies. She'd somehow known that. 'Sometimes just talking something through can help,' she said softly.

'There's no point.'

'You prefer to keep working through your never-ending "to do" list?'

'That's right.'

'And "Take Kassie's virginity" is just another item on that list?'

'Yes.' He squared his shoulders. 'You offered me a deal, Kassie. It's time to make good on it. You need to go and get dressed before we attend the unveiling of a local sculpture. You have two hours before your presentation to the world as the newest adjunct to the Palisades royal family.'

'The *pity* relation, you mean.'

He glanced at the watch on his wrist. 'I'll meet you in my library in ten minutes and introduce you to the stylist.'

She fled, desperate for a cold shower. Then she quickly tugged on jeans and a tee and prepared to swallow all her pride and embarrassment about using the services of a *personal grooming assistant*. She'd spent all her life dressing to disappear into the background, to avoid the eyes of men. But this time… She wanted *him* to notice.

The assistant was waiting with Giorgos when Kassie entered the room fifteen minutes after she'd left him at the pool.

'Meet Thea,' he said, his remoteness fully restored. 'She'll help with your hair, make-up, clothing—'

'I hope you're quite the magician.' Kassie forced a smile, battling her shock at the impassivity Giorgos could summon so effectively. 'I'd love you to help—especially with my hair. It's so thick I—'

'It doesn't need cutting,' Giorgos interrupted roughly.

'Okay, well…' Kassie bit the inside of her cheek, refusing to blush. 'Perhaps Thea and I should go and make our plans somewhere we won't be a bother to you.'

Giorgos glared at her. She met his hard gaze defiantly. As if she'd let him dictate about something so personal! Wordlessly, they clashed for two seconds too long. Then he nodded curtly and turned back to the papers on his desk.

Kassie gritted her teeth, barely restraining a growl at his mute dismissal. The guy was unbearably arrogant.

'I'll show you the way, Ms Marron,' Thea said smoothly.

Kassie jumped. She'd almost forgotten the woman was actually there. But if the stylist was at all curious about Kassie she hid it well. Her assessing gaze held nothing but professional interest as she led her to another guest suite, in which an assortment of luggage and garment bags were waiting.

'I've brought a selection of clothing in a variety of sizes. I wasn't sure… You're not as tall as the Princess.'

'No.' *Not as willowy. Not blonde.* 'Much shorter. Rounder in places.' Kassie couldn't stop mumbling.

'Yes.' The woman nodded. 'And I know exactly how we'll emphasise those assets.'

Panic hit. Kassie had deliberately never emphasised anything. But she remembered the teasing in Giorgos's eyes and her determination to surprise him roared back. Thoughtfully she studied the stylist herself—she was beautifully attired, completely professional… This woman wasn't going to let Kassie out in public looking anything less than 'perfectly appropriate'. Her career depended on it.

So she relaxed and surveyed the garment bags with interest. 'What do you suggest?'

Two hours later, feeling well versed in the art of smiling while saying little, Kassie strolled along the corridor to Giorgos's room.

Just outside the door she felt her heart begin to thump, but she pushed on and walked in anyway. He wasn't seated at the desk but was standing looking out of the window pensively.

'Giorgos?'

He turned. Her breathing stalled—not in anticipation of his reaction, but because of her own impossibly powerful response to the sight of him. He wore another suit, so sharp her eyes watered. Tall, lean and purely predatory, he regarded her silently. For a half-second she was tempted to turn and run. But the fire in his gaze froze her in place.

'Ms Marron.' Slowly he walked towards her. 'You look…'

She waited, but he didn't finish.

Heated amusement—*satisfaction*—trickled through her. 'I've rendered you speechless.'

'Mmm-hmm.'

He stopped right in front of her. Too close for her to remain cool or rational or breathing.

'You're not good at talking at the best of times,' she whispered.

'I talk.'

'Niceties and nothingness—with barriers up all the time that you don't let people past.'

'Are we on *this* again? What do you want to know everything for?' he answered equally softly. 'You're a physiotherapist, not a psychiatrist. And I am *not* one of your patients.'

Fair enough, she supposed. 'You want intimacy without intimacy?'

'I just want *you*,' he muttered bluntly.

Her heart beat heat throughout her body until she was melting. She breathed slowly, welcoming the delicious feeling he brought to life within her.

I just want you.

In the end, what did it matter if that was all there was? Because there was only *now*.

'Message received.' She smiled at him. 'And ditto.'

His face lit up. 'Twirl for me.'

'Pardon?' She paused, eyebrows raised.

'I've paid for the make-over—I want to appreciate the full result.'

The urge to defy him bit, but she kept her eyes on him. And kept her cool. Because a snap back was what he wanted. She didn't know why he'd decided to bait her, but the hunger in his eyes was unmistakable. So was the edgy awareness. Was he testing her? She realised that perhaps this might be more uncomfortable for him than for her. Perhaps she too could play with provocation.

So she forced back her embarrassment and bent her head oh-so-meekly. 'Certainly, King Giorgos,' she acquiesced breathily as she turned slowly. 'She buffed my skin,' she added in a soft whisper over her shoulder. 'All over. So I've not a hair out of place. I guess I'm polished enough for you to be seen with now.'

'Vixen,' he accused huskily. 'You enjoyed it.'

She shrugged and studied her highly polished fingernails. 'I've had harder mornings.'

'And you're enjoying my reaction to the result.' He cocked his head, a rueful light entering his eyes. 'Everyone will look—are you sure you want their eyes on you?'

'They'll look anyway eventually—when I come out of hiding. At least if I'm with you they'll keep their distance.'

'There might be speculation, but I believe I can offset that.'

Her pulse raced too quickly at his appraisal. 'Speculation about what?'

That smile returned—the rare, all too wicked one, full of carnal intent. The one that made all her senses dizzy.

'How do you offset it?' she asked unsteadily.

'I play up the protective angle. Apparently I'm good at that.'

'*Too* good,' she answered tartly. 'And *I* don't get to offset it at all?'

'I won't let them come after you,' he muttered, almost as if he were convincing himself.

'Of *course* they'll come after me—at least for a bit,' she scoffed. 'The dress doesn't matter. I'm not from the right side of the tracks or the right layer of society… They'll talk about my mother—'

'What will they say about her?'

She paused. 'That she was John Gale's mistress for twenty years. A shameless temptress who never truly succeeded in stealing the man she wanted.'

'Why did she wait for him for so long?'

'Because she was weak.' Kassie shrugged sadly. 'You should have seen her when he told her he was coming for one of his visits. She'd dance around, she'd dress up… And then he'd come, and he'd swing me around for a moment, and then they'd disappear to her room.' She frowned, remembering the loneliness that she'd felt then. 'There was no real relationship between them. No romance. There was him turning up to take her to bed and then her bottoming out when he left again.'

Her mother's mood swings had been wretched. But then she'd rally and they'd go on happily together—until her father called again.

'She always waited, believing in him, never moving forward. She always welcomed him back despite that disappointment time and time again.' She'd never understood why.

'You're angry with her?'

'Because she didn't fight for what she wanted. Because when she got sick she didn't fight that either.' She had been so passive, accepting so little. Kassie was never going to do that.

'So are you going to fight for what *you* want?'

'Don't I already?' She lifted her head. 'Aren't I doing exactly that now? I know what I want—from my job, from you and from this one performance in front of the world now. This is on *my* terms, Giorgos.'

'Good for you,' he said, glancing away from

her. 'Hopefully they won't delve all that deeply into your background. It's not uncommon to be illegitimate now. Or to have been raised by a solo parent. That stigma has eased.'

Maybe for normal people—but Eleni and Giorgos weren't anywhere near normal…they were royalty.

'Yet times haven't changed enough for our King to consort with a commoner?' She smiled at him sweetly. 'He still has to find himself a princess.'

'Some things just can't be changed.' He shrugged.

'And you don't *want* to change them,' she challenged softly. 'You've kept everything the same since your father died. So full of tradition you hardly consider your future.'

'Because it is important to honour our forefathers,' he said, stiffening.

She paused, realising she'd touched a wound. 'You must have loved him very much.'

'I only wish I had told him so when he was alive.'

'How old—?'

'Seventeen. I was seventeen when he died.' He pre-empted her question sharply. 'Seventeen and stupid.' He turned away from her. 'We need to leave.'

* * *

Giorgos hadn't made such a massive mistake in a long, long time. Allowing himself to get sidetracked by something personal… Allowing himself to think he could have a moment of fun alongside the execution of his duty… What had he been *thinking*?

He hadn't, of course.

Bringing her with him had been total madness, because he couldn't concentrate for looking at her. In that simple white dress, with its perfectly demure neck and hemline, she was the epitome of sensuality. No gilded artifice required. Her hair had been left loose—it hung in a glorious, glossy swathe down her back—and her make-up appeared minimal. Her lips were not coloured, but their natural rose-pink had been intensified somehow, and her skin was flawless and glowing.

All he wanted to do was kiss her. He shouldn't think about the traditional significance of the colour of her dress, but he was too sharply aware of her innocence and inexperience…her sweetly sultry desire for his touch. The primal pleasure he got from knowing it was only he who'd touched her—who had aroused that begging, writhing wanton—set his teeth on edge.

He ached to return to the Summer House so he could slowly strip her bare. He'd waited long enough. Teased her enough. She was ready and he was too far gone to care about the risk any more. He just wanted her. *Now.*

Thank heavens he'd retained enough nous to ensure that this public appearance would be a brief one—a quick stop to unveil a new sculpture in the garden of a nearby gallery. He'd say a few words, drop the curtain on the marble, smile and leave. She'd be on show for thirty minutes or less, if he could manage it. He just had to manage his own mind. His own emotions. His own damn body.

He was utterly, painfully conscious of her walking beside him into the gallery's garden. She was staggeringly beautiful. He saw eyes widening and jaws dropping as they passed the gathered guests. There were more people lining the street than usual. Of course there were—they wanted to see how things stood since Eleni's marriage announcement. The curiosity in the crowd flared—murmurs, questioning tones lifted as they stared in fascination at the exquisite woman accompanying him.

He shouldn't have brought her. He shouldn't

have used her in this way. He should have kept her hidden. *His.*

She was silent as she walked. Shy. His hand itched. He longed to take her hand in his—to shield her from the intense interest of the invited dignitaries and members of the public. But he couldn't—he'd embarked on this selfish plan and it was too late to turn back. He was careful not to touch her, hardly to look at her. Not to give the wrong impression or let anyone suspect how desperately he wanted to declare his possession of her.

The urge to reach out for her was so intense it sent him off balance. Distracted, he could hardly focus on the short speech he'd prepared. He couldn't stall them the way he'd intended to. His mind blanked—because all he could think of was her. In the end he was forced to admit the discomfort of this situation as he introduced her to the waiting media and the world.

'Ms Marron needed some space away from the scrutiny of the press currently camped outside her home,' he announced through gritted teeth, making them aware of his displeasure at her treatment. 'That is why she is my guest for a couple of days. She's a private citizen and must not be hounded. Naturally she is delighted for her brother and Princess Eleni, but I insist that you respect her privacy. We welcome *all* of Damon's relatives into our family. Any questions must be directed to me.'

'Where's Prince Xander?' a reporter queried.

'Prince Xander has returned home.' Giorgos fought to keep his message on track. 'He is a gentleman, and I must stress that all blame for Eleni's earlier heartache lies squarely at my feet. However, she has forgiven me, and we now move forward together as a family.'

Eleni hadn't wanted him to be labelled a bully. But he knew he deserved the discomfort of this grilling—and that he shouldn't have dragged Kassie into it. He was acutely aware of her standing beside him now, quiet and beautiful, and he just knew she was expecting him to deliver. He damn well would.

'Where is the Princess now?' another reporter asked. 'When will we meet Damon?'

'Princess Eleni and Mr Gale have gone away for the privacy they need at this special time. I may not always show it, but I do understand that they are in love.'

Something rough tickled his throat and it tightened, making speaking even harder. He glanced briefly at Kassie and caught her beautiful, genuine smile at him. He forced his eyes front again, an unnamed emotion firing through his blood.

'Rightly or wrongly, I have always tried to protect my sister and I am very pleased she has found happiness. It is…' He cleared his throat awkwardly, wishing like hell he'd cancelled this appearance, because this was one truth he was suddenly compelled to admit to the world and it was *hard*. 'It is all I have ever wanted for her.'

Kassie dragged her gaze from Giorgos and looked over the crowd in front of them. For a moment there was complete silence, and then a wave of audible support spread—culminating in a huge cheer. This close, Kassie could hear the individual murmurings of the shiny-eyed, smiling women.

'He's so handsome...'

'He's so protective of Eleni...'

'What a brother...'

For the first time that she could ever recall he'd come across as all 'Giorgos' and not pure 'King'—a hurt, caring man, not a dignified, remote figurehead. And she was just as touched as everyone else present.

She quickly glanced down, hoping to hide her burgeoning emotions and the deepening fascination she had in him.

A few moments later he unveiled the sculpture to more applause. The rest of the visit passed in a blur of smiling faces and respectful distance. But she was conscious of intense scrutiny. So many people were watching her, listening, *judging*. But she didn't care what they thought of her—she just wanted to ensure their support of their King.

She didn't want to let him down, so she quietly expressed her gratitude to both King Giorgos and Princess Eleni whenever she was asked for a comment. And then it was all over. One of Giorgos's assistants escorted her to the car. Then Giorgos himself settled in beside her. There was no word from him, no shared look or laugh, and certainly no touch. Fine by her. Their intimacy was her secret to treasure. Her choice.

But even as they drove away from the crowds his distance didn't lessen. If anything, he seemed to become more remote. He sat silent, unsmiling and stiff, staring out of the window away from her. She couldn't think why his frown had returned when everyone there had looked happy. She'd heard the bubbling chatter of approval after he'd spoken and the rising inflections of excitement and support. How could he not be pleased?

She didn't dare speak while the driver might hear them, but she couldn't resist watching him, looking so *correct* and so regal in his fine suit. So on edge.

Only once they were safe inside the gates of the Summer House did he turn his head and catch her staring—but still he said nothing.

Her heart pounded—had he changed his mind? Didn't he want to do this with her any more?

Kassie walked ahead of him into the building, marching straight to the private lounge he liked. Once there, she turned to him, determined to breach the defences he'd put up. 'You won them over. Completely.'

He shrugged off his jacket and undid his tie with rough gestures that revealed his irritation. 'I talked too much.'

'No, you didn't.' She was surprised he'd think that—he hadn't said all that much at all. And what he *had* said had been lovely. 'You were honest with them.'

Her heart stopped as she realised how emotional he actually was at this moment.

'Do you feel vulnerable?' she ventured softly.

He stared at her moodily and didn't respond. That silence, that look, told her the answer.

'Everyone does sometimes,' she said. 'Feel vulnerable, that is.'

'I am the *King*.' He paced away from her with leashed strides. 'I'm not supposed to be…'

'You're still allowed to be human. What's wrong with coming into this century and showing some emotion? It makes you relatable.'

'I don't need to be *relatable*,' he snapped. 'I just need to do my duty.'

He truly thought that was all he was meant to do? That upholding the crown was all he *could* do?

'What happened to work-life balance?'

'There is no difference between the two. My work *is* my life.'

'Why be such a martyr, Giorgos? What sins are you paying for?' She now understood that he really did carry some terrible burden of guilt.

'Back off, Kassie.' He looked lethally angry as he suddenly stalked towards her. 'You don't get to pry.' He reached out and grabbed her. 'What you get is *this*.'

CHAPTER SEVEN

HIS KISS WAS a merciless exposition of unleashed passion. Forcefully he swept her into his arms. Thrills flickered along her veins as she braced herself to withstand his ruthless onslaught and tried to kiss him back. He pulled her closer, bending her back until she was on the very tips of her toes, utterly at his mercy. And she loved it. Electrified, energised, she moaned at this intoxicating bombardment of pure pleasure to her body—and her soul.

With a curse he suddenly pulled back, releasing her and rubbing his hand over his face as he visibly tried to recover his self-control. She didn't want him to—she'd adored the desperate way he'd devoured her, as if he couldn't kiss her enough to satisfy his need. Not ever enough. Which was exactly how she was feeling. The deepest longing had been unlocked within her and she couldn't stand to have it denied now.

'Why are you stopping?' Dazed, she clutched at his shirt so he couldn't stride away from her.

'I'm too rough…' he groaned, but his hands automatically shaped her hips again, as if he were losing his inner battle for control. 'I'm sorry I snapped.'

She liked his emotion—his passion. It meant he was feeling something—the same way she was. *Feeling*, she'd decided, was a good thing.

She shook her head. 'Not too rough.'

'You're not used to a man's touch,' he said huskily. 'There were moments last night and this morning when I might have… I don't want to hurt you.'

'I liked it. *All* of it. I want more,' she said with ferocity, every last inhibition burned away by that kiss. 'I know it might hurt a little…' She huffed out a heated breath. 'I'm certain it'll be worth it.'

His breath whistled through his clenched teeth and his eyes locked with hers. Satisfaction and anticipation drummed louder and louder within her as she read that desire—that decision—within his blazing gaze.

He extended his hand and she laced her fingers through his. Together they walked across the smooth wooden floor to her bedroom.

It was mid-afternoon, so there was no dark night to hide behind. The window overlooked the blue waters stretching to the far horizon. Nothing broke that blue view of sea and sky. The room was light and fresh and utterly dominated by the wide bed.

Heat burgeoned inside her. She ached to lie on it with him, to feel him entwined with her, to feel his weight…

He stopped in the centre of the room and she stood before him. Again their gazes met and melded, the wordless communication heralding the intense connection that she knew they both craved. Slowly he moved, finding the hidden zip of her pretty dress. She held still, held her breath as he released the zipper and pushed the soft linen from her body, leaving her clad in only her underwear.

He unbuttoned his shirt, swiftly discarding it. He reached into his trouser pocket and pulled out a handful of small foil packages and cast them across that ready bed. Then he scuffed off his shoes, removed his socks and trousers, and finally allowed her the satisfaction of seeing him the way he could now see her—almost bared. And so intimate.

Her mouth watered and her lips tingled with the

need to kiss every inch of the skin she could now see. Her fingers trembled, itchy with the desire to coast over his body—to caress and test the muscles that were so sharply defined. She saw his abs ripple as he flinched at her involuntary mumble as she feasted on the sight of his strained black boxers. A hot feeling pooled at the apex of her thighs. She wanted everything. And she wanted it now. But she was too tense with anticipation even to move.

He stepped forward and kissed her and her paralysis ended. She skimmed her hands over him, suddenly bold and hungry. He walked her backwards until her knees hit the bed. Trusting him implicitly, she let herself fall and he came with her, their limbs tangling in a frantic mass of desire. Her need to touch and kiss and lave was uncontrollable.

Inexorably, however, he caught her close and stilled her with the most carnal kiss of her life. He released the catch of her bra, his expression hot as he peeled the silk and lace from her burning skin. She'd never felt as aroused, nor seen anything as erotic as the look on his face as he tugged her white panties down her hips and revealed her sex to his seeking tongue.

She arched up instinctively at the first sweep. He growled in primal satisfaction as he tasted her readiness and her heat. Gripping her undulating hips with one hand, he held her where he needed to so he could continue that intense torment. As she writhed in hunger he fed her—one finger, then two, pumping her, priming her for his full possession. Fastening his lips to her, he feasted, flicking his tongue until she screamed with incoherent bliss. And as the ripples of her orgasm ebbed he kept his fingers plumbed deep, looking down at her ravenously.

He wasn't satisfied yet. And nor was she.

He released his thoroughly intimate hold on her and reached for protection. In seconds he'd stripped off his underpants and rolled a sheath down over his straining, massive erection. Her heart thundered. He was so huge, so stiff. She wasn't sure she could take him…

But she *wanted* to. She couldn't hold still for the wanting.

His eyes on hers, he gripped her restless hips with both hands. Then he bent his head low again. Another luscious lick of his tongue spiked her pulse even more. She knew he was preparing her, but she couldn't wait any more.

'Giorgos…' Her wanton craving was audible.

He stilled, then moved up her body to brace himself above her. So close. She stared up at him, so intensely longing. So trusting.

He held fast, rigid above her. 'There's no going back.'

She didn't answer—didn't want him to give her yet another chance to change her mind. She ran her hand through his silky hair and pressed, drawing him down so she could kiss him the way he'd taught her. Elation soared as he gave her his tongue. But he still held that most masculine part of him an inch away from where she was burning with heat and want.

So as she kissed him—as she welcomed the teasing plunge of his tongue into her hungry mouth—she arched up, rubbing that desperately aching part of her against him. She moaned as she moved, discovering just how much she liked rubbing against him like this. And at last he moved—only the slightest push of his hips to press the thick head of his manhood against her slick sex, sliding between her folds only an inch before slipping back.

Her breath stilled as she assimilated the sensations and again he pressed. And then again.

Gentle, shallow pulses that started to drive her wild. Suddenly she was swamped in the hunger for more—for *all.*

'Giorgos…' she breathed in pure mindless desperation. 'Please. Oh, please. *Please.*'

His sudden fierce thrust breached that thin barrier, plunging him deep into her narrow channel. She cried out at the enormous pressure that gave her both physical fullness yet also intense relief. He was *there.*

'Kassie?' He gazed deeply into her eyes, searching, questioning, wanting.

It was so much more than she'd imagined it would be. *He* was so much more.

'You're hurting?' he asked hoarsely.

'No… Yes…' she whispered honestly, and drew in a shuddering breath. 'No… It's just…'

He kissed her—a sweet, hot kiss—so that for a moment she was too stunned to be able to answer. But then she softened, relaxing into him, her body gradually accepting the possession of his.

And it was so good. She moaned as he began to move, spectacularly slowly. Giving her time to adjust to more…and then more. And then she moved too—experimentally mimicking that delicious rocking of his, interleaving their most sensitive places…

His hands swept over her, skilfully seeking other spots to tease, to treasure. He made love to her mouth, then her neck, then arched above her to tug with divine torture at her breasts while ploughing deep into her womb.

She gasped. That initial shock had now faded, leaving rapture to rise in the driving exertion of his body over hers. He was around her, over her, in her, and he left no part of her untouched. She moaned again as the physical was transcended and white-hot emotions bubbled as he worked her harder. She swept her hands over his chest and then gripped his shoulders, instinctively curling her leg around him to hold him close, urging him.

He met the unspoken desire—the challenge—and took her harder, higher. She panted as the sensations began to spiral, her breathless groans stoking his speed and attention until she cried out in complete orgasmic agony. And then, as waves of ecstasy rained through her body, he released his own—thrusting with unrestrained, unrelenting might before powerfully straining as hard and as deep as he could, spilling his seed into her greedy, clenching heat.

Long moments later he levered himself up from where he was slumped over her to kiss her—a lazy, intimate, generous kiss that somehow bolstered her. She'd been torn apart, and now his luscious, long kiss put her back together. She was reformed. Different. Better.

She sighed with utter contentment as he rolled to his side and then pulled her to rest against him. She felt as if she was floating. 'I had no idea,' she whispered in wonder. 'I just had no idea.'

His answering smile was the most beautiful thing she'd ever seen. She smiled back, wide-eyed, as the aftermath of such intensity fired adrenalin around her body. She couldn't believe what had happened. Couldn't believe how powerful the feeling had been. Couldn't believe her heart would ever settle again.

He suddenly moved, standing up from the bed to turn and scoop her into his arms. He carried her to the bathroom, flicking the lever so water flowed from the multiple jets in the shower. She trembled as he set her on her feet. She was so keyed up by what had taken place. By what she'd felt. By the need to feel it again—to make sure it hadn't been a dream or a fluke… She needed—

'Breathe,' he said softly, placing his hand on

her chest and feeling the frantic beat of her heart. 'Just breathe.'

He carefully lathered her body, massaging her all over with annoying gentleness, but there was a wicked smile lurking in his eyes when he caught her gasps and he took extra time to wash her breasts and down her belly.

She put her hand on his wrist as he was about to step away. 'I want to do it again,' she whispered boldly, her heart still beating that frantic tattoo.

'I know.' He wrapped her in one of the luxurious bathrobes and picked her up again.

'I am capable of walking.' She felt embarrassed, but at the same time she loved the care he showed.

'I like holding you,' he answered bluntly. He paused for a second in the room, and then placed her on the sofa instead of the bed. 'Wait here a minute.'

She wondered what the problem was, but then she saw the bloodstain on the sheet and felt her blush burn. But there was an odd sort of pleasure too—that there was a mark of what had happened. That it had been no dream. It had been earthy and raw and *real*.

'I'll take care of it.' His voice was a little hoarse.

He left the room for a few moments, before returning with a pile of folded linen in his arms. In two seconds he'd bundled the soiled sheets and wafted a fresh sheet over the big bed. She walked over to help him.

'Uh-uh.' He shook his head. 'You'll mess up my corners.'

So she stood back, her arms folded as she watched him work. 'I'm impressed.'

'You thought I was too spoiled to know how to make a bed, didn't you?' he jeered at her. 'I wasn't about to order my staff to come and freshen the place. I'm not *that* much of an ass. I'm—'

'Considerate. Tender. Tough—in a good way,' she interrupted with a smile. 'And you really *do* know how to make a bed.'

'When I was first crowned I realised I wasn't anywhere near ready to take it on and I needed some discipline and order to my day. So I trained with my soldiers. And I make my own bed. Every. Day.'

'Impressive.' She chuckled at his self-mocking smile.

'But I'm not disciplined at *all* now.' He tugged her back down to the bed.

It was true, he realised. He no longer gave a damn about anything in the world other than pleasing Kassie. Sex was always enjoyable, but what he'd just experienced with her had been something else again. The honesty of her response… The unfettered enjoyment… He'd worked so hard to pull that from her. Pleasuring her had mattered to him in a way it had never mattered before.

He was always a considerate lover, and liked to ensure his partner's satisfaction, but he'd wanted the next level for Kassie. She deserved that—so sweet, so lonely. She'd been trembling like a leaf in the shower just now, and a huge wave of tenderness had risen within him. And her flush when they'd returned to the bedroom and seen that rumpled bed…

The most appalling Neanderthal satisfaction rippled through him at being her first—her only—lover. And he was going to do it again. And again. And he was determined to make it even better for her every time. He cared deeply about her experience. And realising that made his muscles tense.

'You're the most disciplined person I've ever met.' Her mouth formed the tiniest, most feline smile.

Another feeling rushed in—all intensity as he registered her blossoming confidence. That smile—that mouth of hers—was going to be the death of him.

He grabbed her hips and hauled her close, wanting to drown in the sensations she aroused within him and not analyse them any more. He kissed her, drawing in her sweet enthusiasm as she wriggled beneath him. His heart thundered as he touched her—she was so warm, so generous, so gentle.

'I don't want to have to do it any more,' he confessed in the intense relief of holding her.

'Do what?'

Resentment—rebellion—burned within him. What he *wanted* would always come second to what was *required.* That was the price he would always pay. 'Pretend to be so bloody perfect.'

'You don't *pretend.*' She frowned up at him. 'In what way are you *not* perfect?' She mocked him with that bewitching smile. 'You're handsome. Intelligent. And you've introduced me to the most magical experience ever. I'm working very hard not to fall for you, my King.'

He stiffened at her admission—even though he knew she was teasing, just to make him smile. But she didn't know the truth of him. Not the raw, ugly facts. Suddenly he wanted her to—so she no longer saw him as a poster boy for the monarchy. He wanted her to understand the poison of his past. And then—selfish, greedy bastard that he was—he wanted her to still want him. He wanted her to look at him with those desire-drenched eyes even when she knew how false he really was.

It felt like a betrayal for her not to know the truth when she had been so honest—so genuine and generous—with him.

'Your original opinion of me was an accurate one, Kassie,' he said, his throat tightening as he rolled to his side to face her. 'You saw straight through me to the truth.'

She stilled at the solemnity in his tone. 'I was defensive and on the attack and I judged you without thinking it through,' she said softly. 'But your mother died in childbirth… No wonder you were worried about Eleni. And Damon's father abandoned his lover in her hour of need… I can understand why you're wary of him.'

'Those things are true—and relevant to a point. But they're not the reason I've wanted to protect her too much for too long.'

'No?' Her eyes deepened. 'Then what's the reason?'

He glowered at her. He didn't deserve her adoration. And the toxic baggage he'd been shouldering alone for years would wipe it out. She wouldn't like him anywhere near as much once she knew. And that could only be a *good* thing. She might have claimed from the outset that she wouldn't get hurt, but hormones would come into play. The gentle warmth in her eyes when she looked at him told him she was too soft towards him already. The truth would burn back any building tenderness she felt for him.

He could only hope the desire would still remain.

'In my teens, I was even more arrogant that I am now.' He laughed, mocking himself. 'Of *course* I was. I could have almost any woman I wanted. It went to my head. Young, sexually adventurous… I didn't think about the consequences. I was having too much fun, and I was arrogant enough to believe I could do anything. Have anything and anyone. I was totally spoilt and I thought I was invincible. Nothing bad could befall me.'

'And then your father died.'

Those eyes deepened again in sympathy. But his sweet lover wasn't as clever as she thought.

'My hedonism killed my father,' he said bluntly. 'His death was *my* fault.'

'It was a car accident.'

'Caused by me. I got into trouble. Serious trouble.'

She drew in a sharp breath. 'Gambling? Drugs?'

'One of my lovers fell pregnant.'

Kassie's mouth formed an 'O'. 'Did you love her?'

'I was almost eighteen. She was nineteen. I thought I'd been careful. I was voracious, but I wasn't stupid. But contraception isn't infallible.'

He hadn't answered her question.

'We weren't in a committed relationship. We weren't exclusive.'

Her expression shadowed. 'So what happened?'

'She was in a panic, and frankly so was I. Her parents were traditional and she was scared.'

'Was she a princess?'

'Aristocratic. It wouldn't have been the perfect match, but it could have been made acceptable.'

'So it wasn't a forbidden love story?' She looked away from him.

'Not for me, no.' He sighed. 'We slept together only a couple of times. For me it was only ever a couple of times with each woman.'

'Tick one off and then move on to the next?'

'Exactly.' He sighed again. 'She was in my

party circle. I slept with most of the women in that group.'

'*How* did I not know you're really such a man whore?'

He looked ruefully at her. 'I might've still been a schoolboy, but I was really good at sneaking around. I was good at lying to my security handlers. And it was a very small, select circle I was in. Everyone had a reputation to lose. Everyone was discreet.'

And amoral. He'd taken up every offer—and there had been many. In those days he'd devoted himself to nothing but hedonistic pleasure. His father had been absent and busy, his sister a kid in the palace nursery, and he'd thought he was invincible and entitled. He'd been an out-of-control brat.

'So what happened when she got pregnant?'

He'd realised he'd screwed up and he had wanted to do the right thing. 'I was going to propose to her. I phoned my father…we had a big fight. He wanted me to pursue a paternity test first. I was angry that he thought he knew more than I did. I wouldn't listen to him. I wouldn't come home.'

He'd been so arrogant, so determined to do what he thought was best and damn his father's opinion.

Kassie's eyes deepened. 'So he came to see you?'

'He didn't usually drive himself, but in this instance… He was speeding…' He closed his eyes so he couldn't see the sympathy in hers. 'He was killed on impact. They said he wouldn't have felt a thing.'

He'd never got over the shock of the soldier knocking on his door.

'It was completely my fault. I killed him.' He was as guilty as if he'd pulled a damn trigger and shot him. 'She wanted to press ahead with the wedding, but I felt I had to do what my father had wanted. I hated it that our last words had been so vicious. Doing that was the least that I owed him.'

He'd been devastated by what he'd done in defying his father's wishes.

'And what was that?'

'A DNA test to determine paternity,' he said grimly. 'It turned out my father's concerns were correct. I was not the baby's father.'

Kassie paled. 'She lied to you.'

'She was scared,' he said dismissively. 'I guess she was going with the safest option.'

Kassie gazed at him, her expression softening.

'You still defend her? Even though she betrayed you?'

'It wasn't like any of us were faithful. And she was young and under pressure.'

'And you *weren't*?'

He paused. He hadn't told her this in order for her to *pity* him, but to push her away for her own good. But now there was a searching look in her eyes that he couldn't withstand.

'I was ripped apart,' he muttered harshly. 'I ruined everything and then I had to stand up for my coronation.'

He'd hated it. He'd known he didn't deserve to hold his head up, let alone wear the heavy gold crown.

'It was all hushed up, of course. No one was ever aware of the real reason why King Theodoros was out driving so fast along the coastal road that night.'

'Oh, Giorgos.' She cupped his face with a tender hand.

'I am *not* the goddamn perfect King.' He jerked free—he didn't deserve such gentle handling. 'Never was. Never will be. I am an arrogant, spoilt idiot who destroyed everything. I was out of control—a guy who was careless with other people's emotions. I was the kind of predatory male you hate—one who liked to score women and didn't give a damn about the mess he might leave behind.'

His skin was suddenly too tight for his body and his heartbeat too hard for his chest. But he saw what he'd wanted to see—the sensual light was still in her eyes.

He shook his head. 'I'm a selfish bastard, Kassie. I'm not worth your time.'

He was a selfish, unscrupulous tyrant who'd manipulated her. *Hell.* He hadn't even intended to. He'd thought his honesty would repel her. But now she was feeling sorry for him, when the last thing he deserved was anyone's pity. But even in this bitter confession he gladly took the comfort of her body because he was so damn selfish. So unworthy. And too damn weak to resist.

'Not true.' Kassie wrapped her arms tight around his chest, holding him to her even as she felt him stiffen as if to pull away.

What he'd just told her was one of the saddest things she'd ever heard. Yet he still defended that young woman. He was still that protective, caring guy. No wonder he'd beaten himself up. No wonder he was so wary for Eleni.

'You tried to do what you thought was right. And you're not that out-of-control kid any more.'

He was far *too* controlled. And it made such sense now. He must have been so hurt—losing his father and then finding out his lover had lied to him.

'What happened to her?'

'She lives in the south of France,' he answered mechanically. 'She's been married for the last six years. Two children now, I believe.'

'That's nice. For her, I mean.'

'It is.' He looked grim. 'You understand now?'

'That you're still beating yourself up for the mistakes of your youth? For things that might have happened anyway? Yes, I see that.'

He'd made allowances for that woman—she'd been young and under pressure—and yet he didn't give himself the same leeway.

'He wouldn't have been on that road—' he began, his hands automatically holding her close.

'But he might have had a crash at some other time. You can't blame yourself. Fate just works how it works.'

'You're wrong.'

'I see people every day who've suffered accidents. Who've lost limbs and lost the lives they used to lead. At some point we all have to accept that life is what it is. Things happen.' She leaned closer. 'Shit happens. But we move on. We accept it and we move on.'

'We can only *truly* move on,' he answered, 'if we alter our actions—ensure that we don't make the same mistakes.'

'But sometimes things are beyond our control.'

'Much is *within* our control,' he argued. 'We're defined by the choices we make. It is *my* duty to uphold the values and the vision of my father.'

This was why he'd changed nothing within the palace. Why he'd become so over-protective of Eleni. Why he'd changed nothing—preserving all tradition. And he'd shut himself down too—not taking any risks. Because he was punishing himself—walking a tightrope all the time, trying to be perfect. Which ultimately—inevitably—was impossible.

'I'm glad she's been able to move on with her life…' Kassie began carefully.

'But you don't think I have?'

'I think you do an amazing job.'

His laughter was not joyous—it was edged in bitterness and mockery. 'Me? The bully? The over-protective tyrant who kept his young sister locked up in the palace has apparently done "an amazing job"? Don't let *pity* blur your vision now, Kassie. Don't think me something I'm not.'

'I know you're loving and loyal, and that you'd do anything for your sister. I didn't understand everything when I first met you.'

'But you were right. I'm selfish and greedy and I like to think I can control everything.' He laughed again. 'Don't worry—I'm not destroyed by the truth.'

'What *are* you?'

He stared at her, considering. Finally he spoke. 'Determined,' he said. 'Determined to take advantage of the freedom that's now between us. You and me, Kassie. This is what it is. And it is *only* this. Only for now.'

He suddenly moved, pulling her beneath him.

'Let's not waste time dissecting things that can't be altered. My past is past. My future is set. There is only this moment to enjoy.' He growled. 'And I'm tired. I'm taking a holiday.'

CHAPTER EIGHT

THREE DAYS. HE'D cancelled all meetings and appearances, citing personal reasons. At the same time he'd released a small statement, informing the media that Ms Kassiani Marron had left the country to seek privacy in Paris for a few days. Their 'alibis' were in place and he was a liar again—a selfish man choosing private pleasure over public duty.

But he couldn't resist. Just this once.

Three days—that wasn't much to ask in return for a lifetime of service was it?

That first morning they'd slept in. He hadn't realised how tired he was, or how incredible it would feel to laze and let time escape as if he had all eternity to spend. They'd floated for hours in the pool, making out, enjoying the warmth and the quiet. Then he'd taken her back to bed.

For the first time in a decade he'd not done his morning training. She'd been sweetly sassy when she'd offered to help him out with another kind of work-out. He'd encouraged her to explore him. To take the lead and do anything and everything she wanted. She'd made the most of figuring out the limits of his strength and stamina. His satisfaction had thrummed as he'd watched her hidden passion blossom. She had a delightful appetite for teasing him.

That pleasure dampened the doubts. Maybe he shouldn't have told her the truth, but he couldn't regret taking the risk. Rather it was a relief, in an odd way, for someone else to know what had really happened back then. It felt like for ever ago. In fact, in this moment, it felt like someone else's life. He finally felt free—as if he'd escaped who he was. Who he had to be. Just by being with her. Just for now. And he wanted it.

So he ignored the caution that licked at his spine every so often. And, as another day slid by, far too quickly, he knew he didn't want to waste any of these moments. There was more to explore with her than sensual gratification. He had other secrets—places to share. And he wanted her to have more from him than just those delicious hours in the bedroom.

She deserved so much more. She was generous and sweet and smart, and he had the pressing need to give her more than that, even if it was only for these few days. After what she'd told him of her parents' relationship, he knew it had been imbalanced. He couldn't offer her a 'normal' dating experience, but he could give her all his time right now—not just in bed. And he wanted hers.

'Why do I need walking shoes?' She raised an eyebrow early on their third morning together.

'So you can walk.'

'Walk where?'

'It's a surprise.'

The small helicopter was ready on the helipad, as he'd requested.

He held the door for her to climb into the front. 'Trust me?'

'Just this once,' she teased, but promptly hopped in.

He took the pilot's seat and looked at her as she strapped up her safety belt. He drew in a steadying breath. 'You really suit that colour.'

'Because I'm a scarlet woman?' she teased as she glanced down at the ruby-red tee that hugged her glorious curves.

'No, you just suit that colour. It brings out the depth of your hair and your eyes—and you're not scarlet. You're passionate and vibrant and the sexiest woman I've ever met.'

'Um… Wow.' Her mouth shut and she swallowed. 'I don't normally wear it—for obvious reasons,' she confessed with a sudden smile. 'But it's my favourite.'

'You should always wear it—but I am not looking at you again for the next half-hour.' He huffed out a sigh and focused, beginning his flight checks. 'I won't get distracted. I've had a lot of training.'

He wanted to reassure her that he wasn't an occasional pilot whose rustiness might put them at risk.

'I'm sure you have.'

Her tone made him glance across at her, despite his vow not to. Her smile was a little sad. 'What?'

'I know how dedicated you are to all that you do,' she replied. 'You never give less than your absolute best, no matter what the situation.'

He didn't reply. He couldn't take that small compliment.

It was only a thirty-minute flight to a mountainous region in the north, where forest-covered peaks rose to touch the sky. He navigated the foothills, steering them through a narrow valley, where he landed on a small flat clearing about halfway up a large mountain that was otherwise inaccessible. Hidden here was a barely visible track, leading up beyond the tree line to the sun-kissed, craggy summit.

'What's the point of the helicopter if we're not going to use it to get all the way to the top?' she asked with a laugh as he pulled on the daypack he'd prepared.

'It's the *challenge*, Ms Marron.'

'Oh, of course.' She rolled her eyes. 'You do like a challenge.'

'As do you.'

He saw her smile in acknowledgement and felt a kick of contentment. He liked reading her, pleasing her. He liked her wit and her teasing. And—red-blooded man that he was—he liked the view as she scrambled up the narrow overgrown track ahead of him.

It staggered him that no other man had taken the time to push past her immediate beauty to the stunning soul beneath. Why had she built those defences so strongly when it was evident—as he'd found as he'd got to know her—that she craved contact and thrived on companionship?

None had been the right companion.

'Why did you really want to go to the hospital ball?' he asked, tension pulling inside him. 'It obviously wasn't because you wanted to meet a man.'

'Actually, I *did* want to meet a man. I had a target.'

'I'm jealous,' he muttered with grim honesty. 'What did he have that made him so special?'

'A research facility.' That teasing note rang in her voice as she answered. 'One of the guests was a researcher. A couple of investors were there as well.'

He remembered she'd told him that now, back on the first night. And to his shame he'd not believed her.

'What research? What did you want to talk to him about?'

'Robotics. They're working on a new prosthetics prototype and I had an idea…' She tailed off.

'And you wanted to share it?'

She nodded.

'Did he like it?'

She turned back to face him, her smile radiant. 'He did. They've been in touch to talk about it more, and they've asked if I want to be involved at the testing phase, with one of my patients.'

‘That’s wonderful.’ But then he frowned. ‘Why couldn’t you talk to him before?’

‘I’ve never had the chance to meet him at the hospital.’

‘Why not? You’ve worked there for years—you’re highly regarded.’

‘As a physiotherapist, yes. Not as a doctor. And this guy was only on Palisades for a few days. So Damon got me in to the ball to introduce me.’

‘That was why Damon went to the ball?’

She nodded. ‘He usually avoids those things.’

Giorgos suppressed a grim laugh—Damon wouldn’t be able to avoid all those palace balls now he’d married a princess. ‘And he had the invitation and the contacts because of his technology companies?’

‘He offered to fund me, but I…’ She glanced up at the steep track and puffed out a breath. ‘I didn’t want that.’

‘Why not?’

‘I don’t want his money. Or anyone else’s. I don’t have the qualifications to work in that area at that level—I just want to share my ideas with the people who are working on it in case it might be useful.’

So she had the ideas, but not the paperwork.

And she was too proud to accept assistance. Irritation prickled the base of his spine.

'I saw a picture of you at that ball,' he confessed. 'If I'd been that man I wouldn't have been able to focus on a word you said because you looked so damned sexy.'

'Well, *he* was polite and *he* did listen,' she said archly. 'And I borrowed that dress from one of the nurses.'

So what she'd said must have been good. 'You should be in on that project.'

She laughed. 'It's not my place.'

'But it's your thinking.'

'Other people are thinking the same. They're the ones who can drive it.'

'While your intellect is wasted and you don't get the credit and challenge you deserve?'

'Not wasted. I do good work with my patients,' she said, defensive pride rippling from her as she straightened to her full height.

'I know. That's clear. But if you have more to offer, then can't you do both? Couldn't you work part-time on the research and part-time as a practitioner? Have you asked if you could?'

'You make it sound so easy.' She shook her head.

'It should be. You ought to be able to maximise all your skills. You should tell the hospital that.'

'It's obvious you're used to making decisions.'

'It's my job.' He paused on the track beside her. 'You initially wanted to study medicine rather than physiotherapy?'

She wasn't as quick with her reply this time. 'Yes, but the training was long and expensive and my mother had got sick. I could complete the physiotherapy course sooner and be a help to her. As it was I studied part-time in my final two years, so it took me longer to finish.'

Part-time because of her mother's terminal illness. She'd been her sole carer. He knew that from the information his team had found. She put her patients—and her mother first. She was determined and proud. But he was determined too, and somehow he'd help her.

That tightness in his chest eased. 'We're nearly there.' He took her hand and led her up the last few steps of the narrow, rocky track until it opened out onto the small summit.

The wind grazed his skin. He liked the hit of oxygen—he was always able to think clearly up here.

'This is beautiful.' Radiant, she gazed across the view.

'Worth the effort?'

'Beautiful moments are *always* worth the effort.'

Something settled inside him in that moment. Peace. She understood. That was what she did—helped create beautiful moments. With him. Probably with her patients too. She looked like a goddess, with her eyes sparkling and her skin luminescent.

Touched, he turned and looked to the horizon, but he kept her hand clasped his. From here they could see right down over the island. The kingdom he'd give his life for.

'I haven't been up here in so long.'

'Why not?'

'Busy.' He gazed across the beautiful landscape and nodded in the direction of the capital. 'Being there.'

'It means everything to you,' she said softly.

'It's what I am.'

'It's *part* of what you are,' she replied. 'But not *all* that you are.'

She was wrong, but he no longer had the desire to argue. He turned and kissed her, reverently drawing from her the response that revitalised his own cold system. Another moment. But that was all.

He made himself move. 'I want to show you something.'

'More than this?'

With a smile he led her to a tussock at the farthest edge of the summit and showed her a small stone cairn that had withstood the wind and now gleamed in the sun.

'Oh…' She crouched down, her smile blossoming. 'You built this?'

He held out a water bottle to her. She took it and sipped while he took a stone he'd brought with him from his pack. With a permanent marker, he drew the date and his initial as she studied the stones already stacked into the mound.

'They all have your initial on them,' she said. 'Doesn't anyone come here aside from you?'

He shook his head. *Not now.*

'Is it forbidden to the public?'

'No!' He laughed. 'I just don't think many people know about it. It's hard to get to unless you have a helicopter and are confident about flying low through the mountain range…' He glanced at the cairn. 'My parents brought me here.'

Kassie knelt to examine the cairn more closely. 'You always bring a stone? Only one each trip?'

He nodded.

'That's a lot of trips.'

It was. 'Right from when I was small.' He should have come more. It always revitalised him. Or maybe it was the woman alongside him who was injecting the energy into his veins.

'A man of tradition.' She smiled up at him, a teasing light in her eyes.

'Is that such a bad thing?'

'Not at all. Not if the traditions don't stand in the way of progress.'

'Most traditions don't. I think they're symbols—connecting us to both past and future.'

He watched as she turned back to study the oldest stones on the bottom of the cairn. Coarse grass had grown, obscuring some, but a couple were large foundation stones. The initials could still be read.

She traced an 'A'. 'Your mother?'

'Antonia,' he confirmed quietly. 'It was her idea.'

'She came here often?'

'It was her favourite place.'

Kassie looked back at the stone. 'Was she lovely?'

'Yes.' Giorgos hunched down beside her. 'My father built the Summer House for her and she decorated it. It was her escape. She'd spend her holidays walking in these hills.' He tossed the stone in his hand and caught it again.

'Her escape?'

Kassie was looking at him with those deep brown eyes. Soft, bottomless, havens of emotion, revealing the caring nature that would be too easy to take advantage of.

'Because she didn't like the palace?'

'No, she did like it, but there isn't much privacy in public life.'

Her gaze skittered from his. 'So your father built the holiday home for her?'

'She spent a lot of time here when I was very young and he was working.'

'It was an arranged marriage?'

'Of course. But it worked well.' His chest hurt. 'They seemed happy to me.'

But his memories were few. He'd only been ten when she'd died.

'You must miss her,' Kassie said. 'It must have been such a shock. No wonder you worry about Eleni's pregnancy.'

He shook his head jerkily. 'With my mother the

complications were unforeseeable and unpreventable,' he said roughly. 'Just unlucky. It's not a hereditary condition. Eleni should be as healthy as any other pregnant woman. She should deliver her child just fine.'

He'd already checked with the doctor.

'That's good.'

It was, but he didn't want to talk about his mother any more—or his father, or his sister, or any of them. He wanted to suspend time and savour this moment with Kassie.

He rubbed his fingers on the rough stone in his hand. 'You should place one to mark your visit,' he said huskily.

Her colour rose and she glanced about, but there were no loose stones on the ground. He'd remembered to bring one from the cave at the back of the Summer House. As always.

'You'll have to share mine.' He uncapped the marker again and with a deft stroke added a 'K' to the 'G'. 'It's tradition.'

He put the rock into position at the top of the pile, carefully wedging one edge of it into a gap between two others, so it would become part of the puzzle. Fixed and stable. It didn't mean anything other than being a record of this moment. It couldn't. But for a long while there was nothing but silence between them.

'We'd better go. The wind here gets cold if you stay too long.' He made himself walk away at last.

She didn't reply as he led the way back down the track. His heart thundered as an empty ache deepened in his bones. He needed to hold her, but he didn't. Because he couldn't let himself *need* to. Instead he forced himself to breathe and focus properly—and not look at her—before beginning his flight checks.

He'd sent his staff away for the day, wanting to be alone with her for every last moment they had left. Wanting one day of a normal, quiet life such as he'd never had.

'Here's the truth,' he confessed as he looked around the kitchen, hoping he could find the things he needed. 'I'm not a good cook. I'm inexperienced.'

'Inexperienced doesn't always equal not good,' she purred.

He chuckled, warmth trickling through him at her sassy confidence—the confidence she'd developed because of *him*. 'We'll have to see.'

'I'm not going to help you.' She leaned against

the bench and sipped the champagne he'd poured for her. 'You'll have to fend for yourself.'

'What do you do at night?' he asked, locating some steak and fresh vegetables. 'You live alone. You don't go out? Have parties?' He sent her a sly look. 'You don't go dancing?'

'You know that already.' She frowned at him. 'Don't tell me *you* dance.'

'Not often. But I know how to.'

'Good for you.'

'Come on.' He laughed at her defensiveness and led her out to the private courtyard. 'You'll never have to dance in public,' he promised. 'Just here with me.'

He seared the steak and the vegetables on the outside grill and they ate simply, but well. Then he put some music on and held out his arms.

Reluctantly she stepped into them, her eyes promising retribution. He didn't care—he just wanted to hold her. He hadn't danced in years. She, clearly, hadn't danced at all.

He was patient, taking the time to show her, to encourage her. It made for moments of laughter—and then she got it. And as the late-afternoon sun faded into night they danced on—little more than swaying together, really—talking of nothing significant and everything important. Silly tales of childhood holidays here that he'd not thought about in years. Anecdotes from his travels and meetings abroad. She countered with stories about her patients.

It saddened him that her life had all been work. She should have had holidays as a child too. But tonight they shared gentle laughter. And then it wasn't so gentle. He wrapped her in his arms and drew her closer still, choosing to forget how transient this had to be—how forbidden it truly was.

But the next morning he woke early, his ability to sleep stolen by guilt and the return of outside pressures. He couldn't avoid his duty for ever. There was no eternity for him.

He tried to ward off the grim feeling, but for the first time the weight of responsibility on him rankled. He wanted more of what he couldn't have. What he didn't deserve. And what she didn't want.

He left her sleeping and swam, but powering through a million lengths didn't work the bitterness from his body.

He stalked inside to discover she'd dressed and eaten breakfast already. She'd chosen a pretty dress, with only her bikini beneath it, and hadn't bothered with shoes. Her long hair was loose and gorgeous, and her kissable mouth was curved into a tempting smile. She was the picture of a summer sweetheart—a holiday fling. But in only a few hours his holiday had to end. His meeting this afternoon was one he couldn't reschedule. And she was due to return to Palisades tomorrow.

The disappointment cut so deep he had to turn away from her. He forced himself to think about work, but he was blocked by an internal shift. Something had changed within him and he couldn't focus properly…

Too bad. He had to. The escape was over.

Kassie noticed him grow quieter and quieter still as the morning progressed. He was withdrawing from her already. He had a meeting this afternoon that was too important to postpone and already he was back behind his large desk, attired in one of those exquisitely stitched suits.

Real life had returned. Their affair was all but over and they were due to return to Palisades tomorrow. So she was determinedly bright. She wasn't going to get melancholic just because time was ticking. She was not going to make any kind of scene.

But the unfairness of it ate at her. She grew angry at the softening inside her. The way she melted at nothing more than the *sight* of him. And she'd seen another side to him in these last days. The serious, uptight King actually *laughed.* He told stories using silly voices. He was open and frank and funny and interested and supportive and tender and a teasing rogue. And that moment on his mountain yesterday… The intimacy she'd felt watching him entwine her initial with his… That had been so unfair of him.

'What is it?' he prompted, looking across at her from the papers he was studying.

Of course he saw everything—as if she was a damn window through which he could see her soul. She hated it that she couldn't see *him* with the same emotional X-ray vision. She hated it that he was the one who could do this—why did it have to be *him*?

'It wasn't just the predatory men I didn't respond to,' she said without preamble, voicing her thoughts without really thinking. 'It was the nice guys too.'

'You mean you've actually encountered nice guys? Not just jerks who lust after your body?' he teased.

'Don't…' She half-laughed. 'I've met a bunch. Some of them were actually okay.'

Probably more than okay. It was just that none of them had spun her wheels.

'I don't know that I'd be as generous,' he muttered darkly. 'Are you saying you've actually had a boyfriend?'

'Almost. I guess…'

'You *guess*?' His gaze sharpened. 'What happened?'

'It was years ago—my first year at college. He was really nice.'

Giorgos put the papers down and looked at her. '"Nice" is an interesting word. But there's not a lot of passion in it.'

'He tried. He was patient. He was caring enough to understand that he needed to go slow…'

'But you felt—?'

'Cold,' she said sadly. And then her 'boyfriend' had got frustrated. 'We never got past kissing. And he was a *nice* guy.'

'I'm sorry.' He stood and walked to the sofa, where she was ignoring the book open on her knee. 'You don't think *I'm* a nice guy?'

She laughed—also sadly. 'I will pander to your ego and make this about you for just this one last moment. You know I think you're more than nice. I think you're amazing. But…'

'But you have buyer's remorse?' His eyes narrowed.

'I just don't understand why it has to be *you* who turns me on.' Her anger got the better of her and the neediness that had been creeping up on her leaked out. 'I don't want it to only be you that can do this to me. It *can't* be only you.'

The one guy she *couldn't* have. Not for good.

His gaze hardened. 'So what are you planning? You're going to go browsing online for a boyfriend? Swipe your screen and match with a bunch of prospects?'

'Really?' She stared at him. Was he *jealous*? How could he get angry with her when *he* was the one who was out of bounds? 'I'm going to go home. Go back to work. And so are you.'

'Just like that?' He snaked out a hand and tugged her to her feet, putting his hands on her hips and pulling her against him. 'You think you're just going to turn this *off*?'

'I've lived without this side to my life for a long time,' she said, bravely squaring up to him. 'I can do without it now.'

The tension between them thickened, revealing the danger in the room—the festering malcontent that she realised he felt every bit as keenly as she did.

'You want to return to your nun-like existence?'

'Why not?' she flared as she felt his steeliness—and his arousal—grow. 'This is just sex.'

Somehow she'd angered him. She paused, anticipating she knew not what. Knowing only that something within him had been unleashed.

'Yeah. It is, isn't it?' He inhaled deeply. 'Turn around,' he ordered.

'What?'

'You heard me,' he snapped coolly, his hands pressing on her. 'Turn around.'

Excitement thrummed low in her belly as she glared at him, their eyes clashing in a battle of wills. In pure challenge. She lifted her chin and then pivoted on the spot.

She heard his hissing breath and his hands shifted. Rough. Fast.

'What are you doing?' she muttered as he walked her forward, his big body insistent at her back.

'Just helping you figure a few things out,' he muttered.

He pushed her forward until her palms hit the wall in self-preservation.

'What things?' she squeaked as he nipped at her neck and then licked the sensitive skin.

'If it's just sex,' he said roughly, pressing behind her, 'there's no need to take our time. No need to get naked. No need to stare into each other's eyes. We can just do it like feral animals. Fast and dirty. Right here. Right now. Get the goddamn release and go.'

His words shocked her. Thrilled her. Because this *was* just sex—that was all it could be. And she was unbearably aroused.

She instinctively used the wall as leverage to push herself back against him. *'Yes,'* she growled, angrily provocative. 'Exactly that.'

She was flattened, rendered immobile, by a hot, furiously hard man. *The* man. Sensual shivers ran down her spine as he flipped up her skirt and yanked her bikini bottoms down to her thighs. Then he grabbed her wrists, lifting her arms above her head and pinning them there with one hand. Delicious pleasure hummed through her body as she registered his passion. His other hand moved back to her hip, holding her hard. Then he thrust, growling as she took him with a gasp of pleasure.

'*This* is what you want?' he asked furiously. 'Me inside you? Me riding you until you come?'

'Yes…' She moaned again, lost to the demands of his body and his words. He thrust hard and fast and relentless, his hot mouth at her neck, his hands holding her fast, his possession total. And suddenly, shockingly quickly, she was right there, her body locked in the rigid paralysis that struck just before convulsions of pleasure.

'You want it from me,' he muttered. 'Any time, anywhere, anyhow. You can't get enough. You like it when I—'

Her scream drowned the rest of his words. She shuddered, her orgasm blinding her. Swift and violent, the waves of ecstasy screwed up every one of her muscles then released her, leaving her limp against the wall. He was still thrust deep inside her, basically holding her up. His breathing was hot on her neck and hard in her ear.

But then he withdrew. She shivered, her legs suddenly weak. He pulled her backwards, into his arms, and carried her to the sofa.

Dazed, she stared up at him as he joined her on the narrow cushions. 'You didn't finish?'

'No,' he answered grimly, gazing into her eyes as he locked back into position inside her. 'Not yet. I want to see you.'

He thrust just as deeply, but more slowly than

before. He framed her face with his hands, looking into her eyes, not letting her turn away as sensations began to pile onto each other again.

'I want to look into your eyes. I want to see when you finally *understand*.'

That connection—chest-to-breast, eye-to-eye—their bodies not just sealed together but interlocked. He kissed her. Working not only to seduce, but to disarm…to overwhelm her.

She shook with the intensity binding them. The ecstasy she'd felt only seconds ago was nothing to the all-encompassing emotion she was drowning in now. It was such a heavenly way to die.

'Giorgos…' She was desperate to breathe.

'You still think this is just sex?'

He was angry with her. She trembled, shocked at the rawness of his question. Angered.

'It's all it can be.' She arched, tormented, arguing even as her body denied her words in its need for him.

'Too late,' he growled. 'This isn't *just* anything. It never was.'

He swept her into the maelstrom of their passion—right into the heart of the storm that brewed beneath the surface whenever they were near each other. She arched again, her body convulsing as it culminated in this—always this—pure, complete bliss.

But this time was different. This time something had been ripped away from them both, revealing stark need and the impossible, hopeless depths of their hunger.

She opened her eyes in time to see him driving hard in that final moment when all his muscles locked and his expression strained in the agony of ecstasy. His eyes were fixed on hers, with deep, wild emotion churning in the fiery green.

He whispered one last word at the moment of release—desperate anger in his demand. *'You.'*

He couldn't bring himself to lift his head and look at her. He couldn't bring himself to return to reality and face what he'd just done. But he couldn't stay crushing her like this on the soft sofa either.

He pulled away from her, quickly standing and adjusting his clothing. He was still completely dressed—his shirt untucked, his skin sweaty. Finally he braved a glance at her. She looked shattered. Her eyes were wide and vulnerable as she silently watched him. Her lips were more swollen than usual. A purplish love-bite stood out angrily against the creamy skin of her neck.

God, he'd been an animal. He had lost all control—just taken what he wanted, held her closer and tighter as he'd driven as deep as he could into her body. He'd lost himself entirely in the pleasure he found only with her.

But she'd been ready—wet and willing—and she'd pushed back on him just as hard as he'd thrust into her. It had been wild and reckless and it had turned him inside out. His orgasm had been the most prolonged and intense of his life.

But wrong. *So* wrong.

Cold, acidic guilt roiled in his stomach. He had just had unprotected sex with her. The one mistake he'd never, *ever* made. But she was the absolute temptation of his life and he'd retaliated insanely at the thought of her leaving. At the thought of her being intimate with some other guy. At her insistence that she would return to her home and this would end.

He'd rejected the notion in an irrational, explicitly physical way. He'd lost utter control—of his emotions, his mind, his body. All he'd wanted was to gorge on the succulent delight of her soft embrace. He'd forgotten his duty—to his crown, to his country, to his father, to himself. And to her.

He froze as the ramifications flashed through his mind.

'That never should have happened,' he croaked formally, struggling to clear the words past his clogged throat. 'I apologise.'

She blinked and slowly sat up, clearly confused as she tugged down the crumpled skirt of her pretty dress.

'I didn't stop to protect you,' he explained shortly.

Her gaze narrowed. 'You mean contraception?'

'I'll send for my physician immediately, to get an emergency contraceptive. There's no need for you to be concerned.'

He couldn't look at her. He couldn't cope with the image in his mind's eye of her pregnant. *Vulnerable.* The risk rendered his lungs useless. He walked away before he threw himself on his knees at her feet to beg her forgiveness. To beg her to… *what*?

'I'll make that call now,' he growled.

Kassie stared as Giorgos retreated behind the grim, forbidding demeanour he'd perfected over the last decade. She felt flayed. He'd just told her this wasn't 'just' sex and then in the next breath proved that that was *exactly* all it was. When cold reality hit—when the possible impact of their affair on the future was raised—he'd wanted nothing more than to reject her and run. The last thing he wanted was a long-term complication.

Well, she could put him out of his misery—even though he'd just thrust her into heartbreak.

'I'm not going to get pregnant, Giorgos,' she said, coldly quiet.

'We just had unprotected sex. Pregnancy happens,' he snapped.

'It wasn't unprotected.'

'What do you mean?'

'I'm on the pill.'

'Pardon?'

'The contraceptive pill. I won't get pregnant.'

He stared at her, clearly shocked. 'Why didn't you tell me sooner?'

'You didn't give me a chance,' she said scathingly. 'You were too busy planning for your doctor to come and save you from possible scandal.'

The truth? She'd wanted to see his reaction to the initial prospect—like the masochist she was. His horror had been unmistakable. Of course it had. He'd actually paled at the thought of her pregnancy. That had told her everything.

'Why are you on the pill when you don't have sex?' He frowned, his tone hostile.

'Don't you believe me?'

'You don't strike me as the type to pump yourself full of medication unnecessarily.'

And yet he'd just directed her to do exactly that—without even *discussing* it with her. He had no consideration of her wishes or her feelings. Had he really thought he could just order her to do as he wanted?

'How do you know it's unnecessary?' She bristled. 'There's more than the obvious reason for taking the pill. If you must know, my cycle is problematic and the pill makes it easier for me to manage.'

'But you've been staying here for the last few days. Did my men pack your pills?'

'When they went through all my personal things?' She was incensed. 'No, they did *not*. Because I keep them with me.' She marched to her bag and emptied it out on the table, snatching up the pack of tablets and thrusting it in his face. 'Here's your proof.'

She watched him. He just couldn't help himself. He had to check, his eye quickly seeing the empty spots in the blister pack. They proved she'd been taking the medication regularly. *He* proved he didn't trust her word.

'You think I'd lie?' she asked softly. 'You think I'd try to take advantage of you?'

He hesitated.

She sucked in a breath. 'I'm not her. You should know that.'

'I just...'

'No. No "just", Giorgos. I've *never* lied to you. I've never tried to trick you. But you still can't trust me.'

It hurt so much more than it should. Because she'd trusted him—utterly. And he'd treated her with such tenderness and respect. Her body, that was. But this was more than physical intimacy now. This was a threat to his future and now his true feelings were on display. He didn't want her—not the same way she wanted him.

Suddenly she realised just how much trouble she was in. How much hurt she was seconds away from suffering.

'I told you *everything*,' he gritted. 'How can you say I don't trust you?'

'You just proved it,' she said quietly.

Would it have been so awful if she'd got pregnant? Obviously to him, *yes*. He'd wanted to get rid of that potential problem as quickly as possible because he didn't care about her. But she…? She felt…

She paced, hiding her face as she realised just how deeply she'd fallen for him. How had she thought she could remain in control and *safe*? Because he was ultimately unattainable? That didn't matter a jot—he'd still got to her. She'd become entranced. Even though he was bossy and decisive and so…so damn strong.

It's just a crush.

He was her first—that was why she felt such a connection, right? But she knew just what a lie that was. It was like being hit by a bus—realising just how hard she'd fallen for him.

'I do trust you,' he said in a clipped voice. 'But I should have stopped,' he said quietly. 'I should have used protection. My anger was misplaced. I was angry with myself.'

'I should have stopped as well,' she snapped back. 'You don't get to assume total responsibility for what happened. It was as much my fault as yours. I knew there was something different. I *felt* it.'

The darkness in his eyes deepened. 'Did you like how it felt?' he asked, ever so softly.

Somehow he'd crowded her. Somehow she was back against the wall and he was right there in front of her.

Her breathing quickened. 'Yes…'

So close. He was so dear to her. And quickly they were back to this all-consuming intensity and desire. But now she knew there was nothing beneath that for him. She couldn't let him close again. Not when he hadn't even apologised for the real hurt—he didn't even know what it was.

'Stop, Giorgos.'

His jaw hardened. 'Why?'

She glanced away from him. 'I have to get back to work. So do you.'

'I will see you in Palisades?'

She stopped breathing. He offered such temptation. But goosebumps lifted. 'No.'

'I'll send for you,' he said urgently. 'No one will see the car under cover of darkness.'

She chilled at his plan. 'And will I leave again a couple of hours later?'

'Yes.'

A booty call?

'No one will know,' he added with arrogant assurance. 'I'm sure we can manage it. I'd build a goddamn private tunnel from your place to the palace if I could.'

It was *that* important that no one knew he was sleeping with her?

'Because I'm that much of a liability?'

He stiffened. 'That wasn't what I meant.'

She made herself breathe. Made herself remain strong for her own future—her own freedom. His acceptance of her in public had been only in her role as the black sheep of his new brother-in-law's family. Not anything else. She wasn't good enough for him to be seen with in a *relationship.* Clearly there was nothing worse than that idea for him.

Initially she'd been fine with their affair being conducted in secret—that had made total sense for them both. But that had been when it was a short-term fling—her lessons in sensuality. But for an ongoing arrangement? *No.*

'I should go now,' she said shakily. 'I want to go *now.*'

'Kassie—'

'We're over,' she interrupted furiously. 'It was only ever going to be these few days.'

That had been her decision. Her terms.

He didn't move. 'I don't want this to be over.'

'It has to be.' She gritted her teeth.

He placed his hands on her shoulders. 'Just a little longer.'

She quaked inside at his touch. 'Just a little longer?' She half-laughed, half-sobbed. 'You can't be serious. What do you want us to do—carry on an affair in secret? Or do I get to become your consort? Your concubine? Do I get to sit around and wait for you for ever and ever?'

'You're putting an overlay on this that doesn't need to be there. You're not your mother—'

'That's right. I'm *not*. I'll never be a kept woman. I'll never wait and wait…'

'I'm not asking you to. I'm not offering false hope—'

'You're asking me to stall my future.'

He dragged in a harsh breath. 'I'm asking you to stay in the present. To let this thing between us run its natural course.'

'Its "natural course"?' She laughed bitterly. 'You mean run until you get sick of me.'

He paled. 'Kassie—'

'So I suspend everything and wait to meet you in secret?'

She knew marriage—love—was never going

to happen. Not for her—not from him. He didn't think she was worth public acceptance—not really.

'Secrecy is to protect you. For your safety.'

'So I don't get judged in the press for being your mistress?' she said scathingly. 'More like so you don't get judged for *having* a mistress,' she snarled, so, so hurt. 'What if I meet someone else?'

She saw the arrogant tilt of his chin at her suggestion.

'What happens when you finally decide to step up to your burdensome royal duty and propose to the perfect Princess?' she asked rawly. 'What happens when you finally choose your wife? What happens to me then?'

He froze. 'That's not—'

'You're happy to waste my time until then?'

'You don't want this to be over any more than I do,' he argued angrily, his fingers tightening on her skin.

'I want what's best for me. And that *isn't* you.'

'You said this was just sex,' he taunted her, that wildness flashing in his eyes. 'You said you had nothing to lose by being with me.'

'You really do want it all from me, don't you?'

She was horrified. 'I might not have had boyfriends, but I've had other relationships—*real* friendships. With patients, with friends at work. I care about people.'

'And I don't?'

'You devote your life to your people, to your duty. But, no, you don't *care* about anyone. I pity you.'

'You don't need to feel sorry for me. I'm not one of your patients with some piece missing.'

'There's a *big* piece missing. In your chest.'

He laughed mirthlessly. 'So now I'm heartless as well?'

'Yes.' Because if he had any kind of heart—any kind of conscience—he wouldn't be asking this of her. He would understand why this was so abhorrent.

'Is it so awful to want to protect you? To care for you?' He cupped her cheek with tenderness, despite the frustration in his voice. 'The secrecy I'm proposing is because I care about you.'

How dared he make it seem that he was offering this for *her*?

'But you don't *want* to care about me—that's the point.' Her anger lit. 'This isn't about me at all. This is about you controlling everything in your life.'

'I *can't* control this,' he growled.

She closed her eyes. 'I refuse to be my mother. I'm not *settling*.' She couldn't wait for a man who was never going to give her what she needed. 'We don't want the same things. We don't *feel* the same things.'

'What *is* it you feel? Desire? For the first time in your life? And you're going to go and feel it with the rest of the world now? *No* man can give you what I can give you.'

'But I don't *want* the little you're willing to give me.'

'Not this?' He hauled her close against his furiously hard body. 'You're going to lie to my face and tell me you don't want *this*?'

Oh, she wanted it. She wanted it almost more than she wanted to breathe. But she would slowly suffocate and starve, because it wasn't enough to sustain her. She'd become bitter and lonely and poisoned by disappointment and emptiness. She'd become sick. Just as her mother had.

'Stop, Giorgos,' she breathed, begging him for reprieve.

He too was breathing hard. In his eyes she saw

it—intention. She knew what he longed to do, the way he would touch her. The way she would touch him back. One blink, one word, and it would happen. She couldn't let it happen.

And he saw.

He blinked something away and stepped back, but not before a parting trail of feather-light fingers down her arms. Torturous…uniquely devious. And then his hands dropped. The farther he stepped away, the more she wanted him to come back.

'This is what you want?' His disbelief was audible. 'To go back to feeling nothing?'

She stayed silent because she couldn't lie.

Never could she accept the little he was offering. He didn't even understand just how little it was. Their affair hadn't helped her embrace her sensuality—it had served only to form an addiction that worsened every time he came near.

'I only want to protect you,' he said.

'That's a lie.' She lashed out. 'This is about protecting *yourself*.'

'You know I don't want you to suffer the way—'

'You could change,' she snapped. 'You could do things differently. You could raise expectations and the public would go with you. You lead—

they follow. But you're too busy punishing yourself for things that happened long ago. And you don't want me enough to fight your need to maintain tradition. To fight for *me*. Not even to try to support me through it. You don't trust me. And you don't love me, Giorgos. And, no, I know you never said you would. But unless things change you'll never love *anyone*.'

'And you *will*?' His anger rattled. 'You think you've got it together more than I do? You've shut yourself off from finding any chance of love. You won't even go out on a date.'

'You're right—I won't. But now I know I need to change. And I need to change *this*—right here. If I'm too busy with you I can never have the chance to meet someone else. To meet the man who *is* right for me. Because it's not you, Giorgos. It'll never be you.'

She dragged in painful breaths and kept pushing.

'And that wasn't a challenge to your arrogant ego—that's just the truth. Because you were right—this wasn't just sex for me. I could have loved you. But you won't *let* yourself be loved. Not by me, or your sister, or anyone. You're not protective—you're arrogant and superior. You don't think anyone can handle things the way you can. But you handle *nothing* of true value. You use your guilt to hide from having an actual life, with real relationships. You have so much more to offer your people. So much more to give of yourself if you'd only set yourself free… But you're too much of a control freak and you're a coward. The truth is you have no intention of loving anyone—least of all *yourself*.'

She broke off, staring at him. She'd gone too far. He was deathly pale, but the wildness in his eyes burned. His breathing was loud and ragged. Slowly the ice returned to his expression. And slowly, with excoriating pain, she realised he wasn't going to argue with her. He wasn't going to fight. This had to be over. She had to leave. *Now.*

'I'm going,' she muttered, with as much dignity as she could muster, and walked out of the room.

He didn't answer. Certainly didn't follow her.

She showered and dressed again, in plain jeans and a tee, only to discover when she emerged from her suite that he'd left for his appointment early. Of course he had.

It was almost another two hours before he returned. Two hours in which she'd had time to plan. And pack.

He didn't come and find her when he returned. She waited for almost half an hour and then ventured to his lair. He was behind his desk, looking as remote as he'd looked that very first day. He watched silently as she approached him.

'I'd like to return to the city,' she said quietly.

'I've said I'm sorry,' he said stiffly.

'I know you are. But we both know this is over. We got carried away.' She lifted her chin proudly, but couldn't look at him directly. 'I've handled all those cameras on me. They've got the only story they're going to get. The interest is only going to die down from here—especially when Eleni and Damon return. I'll be perfectly safe.'

'I insist upon security for you.' He glanced at a sheet of paper on the pile before him. 'I'll make the arrangements.'

Kassie walked out of the room. *Just a crush.* Self-delusion was the only way to maintain sanity through this.

Less than an hour later she locked her hands tightly together in her lap and stared hard at them. She refused to look out of the window as the helicopter flew high, taking her far from him. She refused to cry.

Just a crush. She'd be over it in no time.

CHAPTER NINE

SHE WAS NEVER going to get over it. Three days had passed since she'd left him at the Summer Palace. Three days of no contact. No respite from her bleeding, smashed-up heart. The only way she'd coped was by going to work and pouring everything into her future there. But she could hold it together only so long.

When she returned home it hit all over again. He'd struck where it hurt most, by asking her to be his secret mistress. She'd been terrified of being wanted but not loved—as her mother had been all her life: *wanted* but left waiting, hoping, believing…and it never happening.

Her father hadn't given her mother what she'd deserved. Her mother had loved him wholly, unconditionally, giving him all the best of herself and accepting so little in return. And then, when she'd needed him most, he'd spurned her.

All her life Kassie had been so angry with her mother for that weakness. But now she understood just how much courage it took to love someone—how much bravery was required to put yourself on the line. Now she understood how deeply her mother had loved, however misplaced that love and trust had been, and she could take some pride in her ability to be able to love so deeply and so completely. Kassie could do that.

But her mother had refused to believe she could love that way again. Refused to end it with John Gale and try to start again. And *there* was the mistake Kassie wasn't going to repeat.

Inadvertently, it was exactly what she had been doing before, by not even trying, not even dating. But if she'd learned how to love once, surely she might again? She had to overcome this heartbreak, choose to live. And eventually choose to love again.

It would take even more courage to risk her heart and try again. But the next guy who asked her out… She was going to say *yes*.

Furious, Giorgos stalked the length of the palace and back again. And again. That last argument replayed round and round in his head. His anger didn't diminish—it just grew.

He'd asked her to be with him in a way he'd

never asked another woman to be. But she had pride, didn't she? So much pride. And she had a career. She had a life.

He could give her a better one.

His arrogance mocked him. So too did the newspapers that littered the desk in his private suite.

'The physiotherapist'—the press referred to her that way. They'd investigated her, all right—honing in on the shy, natural way she'd talked to those guests at the sculpture unveiling. Then they'd dug out tales of her rapport with her patients—puff pieces that filled the gossip rags. They'd taken the illegitimate half-sister of the Princess's new husband to their hearts. 'Kassiani the Caring' had replaced 'Eleni the Pure' on the covers of the magazines.

Why did they insist upon putting the women in his life on damn pedestals for worshipping? Making them out to be more than human while at the same time treating them as *less* than human—as only two-dimensional.

Yet wasn't he every bit as guilty of that? Of thinking that neither Eleni nor Kassie could handle all that he thought *he* had to handle?

He studied a clipping about Kassie talking to the guests at that sculpture unveiling. So natural and poised, able to talk to anyone. She'd chosen not to let herself get physically involved with anyone before, but *he'd* been the one battling emotional frigidity. Where she was warm and giving he was ice, refusing to open up. And in doing that he had denied her too. When she deserved so much more.

And she was right. He *was* a coward. Hiding behind his supposed protective instincts to protect *himself*. He was terrified of making mistakes. Of not being good enough. Of not living up to the name he'd been burdened with at birth. Of letting everyone down. *Again.*

Of being hurt.

But *this* hurt so much. And he was so confused.

Her rejection enraged him. As for the thought of her finding another man who could satisfy her needs… That thought just about sent him insane. And that had been the problem. That had been when he'd lost control completely.

Yet when she'd asked him about his future wife he'd gone cold. Marriage was the last thing on his mind. All he wanted was Kassie at his side—in the secrecy of his home. He wanted her to be his alone. His secret. His treasure. He didn't want to share her with anyone. He didn't want her to be at risk or have to perform.

She made him feel so vulnerable. And why was that?

He closed his eyes as the painful truth hit him.

He'd thought he was so controlled. That he'd always done what was best for everyone—as if he was so damn all-knowing. But the only person who'd benefited had been *him*. *He* was the one kept safe.

He'd thought he was playing his role perfectly. Instead he was just a pompous ass. Emotionally lazy and never putting himself at risk. Not in any real sense. Maybe it was time to be the ordinary guy he truly was. The ordinary guy who'd made massive mistakes in the past and who'd just made another one. He'd pushed Kassie away because she threatened everything—his whole ordered world. But the truth was she *was* everything. She *was* his world.

Her words haunted him. *'You can't give me what I want...'*

He'd been too caught up in his own petulant outrage to ask the obvious question—*what* did she want? Initially she'd wanted an affair, but not any more. He knew what she *didn't* want—to be hidden away as his mistress, unacknowledged and having her value belittled…to be second-best to nothing. But he'd done exactly that to her.

He hadn't meant to. He'd been so thrown by his explosive loss of control, so afraid he'd ruined it, he'd wanted to buy some time to explore where this was going in private. He'd felt as if he was on a damn runaway train, and he'd wanted to pull the emergency brake for a moment to catch his breath. But he was a coward—because he'd already *known* where it was going.

She was right. It was time to make some changes. Not just within himself, but within the palace. He would put up a damn painting that *he* liked—one that hadn't already been there for centuries. One of his sister's. How had he been so obtuse as not to even let Eleni put up her beautiful paintings? He'd offered nothing but a total lack of support.

Kassie had put up Eleni's pictures in her office. Kassie had instinctively seen her depths and her value. Kassie saw the good in people—in her patients. She believed in them. She was kind and supportive and caring. All she'd wanted was the same in return. And he'd failed her.

But now he knew how much he needed her—

wanted her. *Loved her.* She was the one—the only one for him. But he'd hurt her. She'd gone into orbit at the thought of being his 'kept' lover, long-term. Of being his secret. He'd retaliated emotionally—irrationally—and she'd wounded him with deadly accuracy.

But how did he become the man she needed him to be? How did he convince her to believe in him now?

He needed time, and a place where they wouldn't be interrupted. And, as much as he wanted to, he couldn't kidnap her a third time.

CHAPTER TEN

KASSIE HURRIED UP the path to her apartment. The security guard that she couldn't get rid of and was secretly grateful for had kept the photographers at bay, but she could barely contain her emotions until she got safely inside. Once in, she dumped her heavy bag, unable to attempt reading the report the senior researcher had sent across that afternoon. Not yet. Not now she was finally alone.

Hurt. She was still so hurt.

Hot tears streaked down her face. She'd been holding it together all day and now she could curl into a ball on the floor and howl her heart out. Again. For the fourth day in a row. When was she going to start feeling better?

A loud knocking on her door made her jump. She froze. She didn't want anyone to see her like this.

'Open up, Kassie, I know you're in there.'

Giorgos? No, no, no.

'Kassie?' He thumped the door again. 'Open up.'

He wasn't being quiet either. Furious, she wiped her eyes with her hands and unlocked then opened the door.

He took up almost all the space. He'd dressed down in jeans and a tee, with a cap tugged low on his forehead, but he was all King. The clothes made no difference. And he was gazing at her with such intensity—none of that regal remoteness in his hot expression.

His mouth flattened as he took in the signs of her distress. 'May I come in?' he muttered roughly.

She wanted to say no. To scream it.

'Of course.' She stepped back politely.

'I've learned not to invade your privacy without permission.' He looked pained momentarily. 'I'm not incapable of learning, Kassie.'

She closed the door but remained in the small hallway, determined not to let him get past the fragile defences she'd whipped into place. 'What do you want?'

He cleared his throat but kept his green gaze right on her. 'I wondered if you had plans for dinner tonight?'

She stared at him blankly. 'Are you asking me…?'

'On a date, yes.' He rolled his shoulders, looking awkward. 'I've never really asked a woman on a date before. You've been asked lots of times, and I know you tend to say no, but I was hoping you might go gently with me.'

She lifted her chin. 'Because this is all about *you*?'

The twisted smile faded. 'This is all about me *and you*. About us.'

'There is no us.'

'There is—there will be. There can't not be,' he said tightly. 'We just need to go gently with each other. I want the time and the space to get to know you. To court you. To do the things normal people do when they're starting a relationship. But unless we date in secret everyone is going to watch. I just—' He broke off. 'I'm just asking for one dinner. One date.'

Kassie stared at him, her pulse drumming. What did he mean by 'starting a relationship'?

'It's not that I don't want people to know we're involved,' he added suddenly. 'I just want us to have the chance to take this further without the burden and pressure of public interest.'

To take *what* further?

'It's not just sex, Kassie. We both—'

'You don't have to do this. I know you don't want to.'

She turned away. She couldn't cope with what she was reading in his eyes. She couldn't trust—

'If you'd let me actually finish, you might find out what it is that I *do* want.'

She glanced back at him.

'I told myself I was wary of scaring you off and coming on too strong,' he said softly. 'Really, *I* was the one who was scared. And you, like me, need certainty and security.'

She couldn't interrupt him now. The lump in her throat was too huge.

'I said some things I didn't mean the other day, and I didn't say the things I should have. My emotions got the better of me and I stupidly thought I could…' He drew in another breath. 'I thought that if we could talk over dinner then we might get somewhere.'

'Dinner?'

'Yes.'

'Where? When?'

'I took a chance and ordered pizza.'

'Pizza?' she echoed numbly.

'It should be here in about five minutes.'

She was lost for words.

'Say yes, Kassie,' he coaxed.

She had the feeling that if she did she'd be saying yes to so much more. And she wasn't ready to do that.

'I'll have some pizza,' she said guardedly. 'But that's all.'

'Great.'

His smile flashed, hitting her all the way to her toes.

'I've thought about this for days,' he said, slowly strolling towards her. 'What to say…how to say it.' His gaze didn't leave hers. 'May I ask you another question?'

'Already?'

She should have known he'd immediately want something more. He was too close. She backed up, but got blocked by the wall.

'Isn't this moving too quickly for a first date?'

He kept walking until he was only an inch away from her. 'You know I can go from merely holding your hand to muffling your screams as you orgasm in less than a few moments.'

Heat flooded. 'You're—'

'Able to be myself around you. Able to take risks that I can't with anyone else. Because I know I can trust you. But you don't feel you can trust me because I let you down. And I'm so sorry about that. Give me another chance. Give *us* a chance.'

She shook her head and pressed her hand on his chest to stop him—but at the same time she was checking he was actually *there*. That this wasn't all in her head.

'Don't use our chemistry to convince me,' she begged him.

'You're already convinced. You know how good we are.'

'It's just—'

'No. It's *not* just sex. It never was.'

'Who's the one interrupting now?' She glared at him.

'I wondered about a public display. A moment of totally open vulnerability. Being that human guy, not the remote, bloodless King… But then that makes it all about me again, doesn't it?'

She stared at him silently, wondering what he was meaning now.

'And it limits your options,' he mused. 'How could you answer honestly if all the world is watching a public proposal?'

A *proposal*? Was *that* what this was? Kassie's legs trembled.

'How could you do anything other than say yes?

Which would work in my favour, I guess—but then, this is you, and you don't tend to do things the conventional way. And besides, I don't want to manipulate you. You need to know exactly what you'd be walking into.'

'What *would* I be walking into?' she whispered.

'Madness. All those cameras. All that judgement. I always said I never wanted to put a woman through that. I watched my mother struggle with it. I wanted to protect my sister from it. I saw all those society women turn themselves inside out and change themselves to try to be someone else… I didn't want *you* to change. But I've realised I'm all too human, Kassie, and I'm completely selfish. I want you. Even though it's not in your best interests.'

'Are you still of the belief that it's up to *you* to decide what is in my best interests?' She stared at him. 'Seriously? You're *still* being overprotective?'

'It's a very hard habit to break.' He sighed, resting his hands on the wall on either side of her as he gazed into her eyes. 'I'm so sorry, Kassie. I'm sorry I let you think I was offering less than all of me. That you thought I wanted to keep you like some dirty little secret I was ashamed of. It wasn't like that at all. It's just that you are so precious to me that I feel scared. I want to lock you up and keep you safe.' He shrugged. 'I'm still working on that urge. The truth is I love you. I was just too stunned to realise it.'

She stared, still speechless, unsure she'd heard him correctly.

'I love you,' he repeated, and this time he smiled as he said it. A tender, wary, but fierce smile. 'I want to be with you and for you to be with me. And all that entails.'

'It's too soon,' she whispered. 'You barely know me.'

'I know you're honest and loyal and funny and serious. I know that you care about people, that you love to help people. And that you're lonely. I know that you deserve to be loved utterly…' He suddenly fell silent and a frown threatened. 'But if you think it's too soon for me to love you…then I guess you don't love me.'

He cleared his throat awkwardly and sucked in another deep breath.

'That's why I'm asking for time. It's what I meant the other day, only I butchered it because I wasn't thinking clearly. I want you to get to know me properly. To trust me again. I can't tell you how sorry I am that I broke your faith in me.'

Deep distress welled up in her. She didn't want him to think that she didn't care. 'I was *scared*,' she whispered. 'I wanted so much more. I'd done exactly what I told myself I wouldn't do.'

'What was that?'

'Fell…' Her eyes filled with stupid tears and she shrugged her shoulders, because she couldn't put it all into words. 'For you…' she whispered.

His kiss was the gentlest thing, and it didn't last anywhere near long enough before he pulled back.

'Here's the thing…' He reached into the pocket of his jeans. 'Tradition dictates the King's bride wears the Cristallino Diamonds. This is the ring and this necklace is part of the set. There's also a tiara to match, but I couldn't fit it in my pocket.'

She blinked at the dazzling waterfall of sparkling stones cupped in his hand—polished, stunning, priceless. Her pulses roared as she shook her head. 'I can't… We can't.'

'Of course we can. I'm the King—I decide. I can marry who I want. And I want you.'

He tossed the necklace and the ring to the floor and framed her face with tender hands.

'You're not exactly disreputable, Kassie. Truth

is, I don't deserve you and we both know it. But while the diamonds are beautiful and traditional, and full of meaning and importance, I want something just for you. *Not* traditional. Not because history says I have to. Just for you. Something that I chose in the hope that you would like it, because even though it hasn't been very long I hope I know you.'

He reached into his other pocket and drew out a small box. He fumbled slightly as he lifted the lid so she could see the contents.

She gasped on seeing the ring resting on black velvet. The ruby was the richest red she'd ever seen—darkly passionate, it almost seemed to glow with an internal fire as it sat snug in its deep gold setting.

'You like it?'

A tear trickled down her cheek as she nodded. 'It's beautiful.'

'Like you.' He took the ring and tossed the box, and gently slid it down her finger. 'Beautiful *inside* as well as out. Hidden fires.'

His hands shook ever so slightly and he wouldn't let her fingers go.

'You don't have to choose,' he muttered. 'I hope you'll accept both. The public will expect to see the diamonds…without them they'll be sceptical, superstitious…but between us… I want this just for you. I want to *be* just for you. I *need* to be just for you. That's what I wanted when I made that stupid offer. For you to be mine. I was being greedy and I didn't realise it. I wanted to have you and protect you at the same time.'

'How many times do I tell you that you don't have to protect me?' Her voice cracked.

'Like you can't help yourself from caring?' He shook his head. 'I can't be something I'm not. You can't ask me to stop caring if I show it in wanting to protect you from a level of public scrutiny that only someone in my position can truly understand. You might as well ask me to cut off my arm. I can't do it.'

She gazed at him. 'We could do it together,' she suggested shyly. 'If you can trust me, I'll tell you when I need you to take me away and we can escape just the two of us to the Summer House.'

He stood very still. 'You'll tell me?'

'You know I will,' she teased, but her eyes filled.

He laughed suddenly. 'Yes. I love you, and I'm quite prepared to spend the rest of my life proving it to you.'

But then he frowned, his grip on her tightening.

'I couldn't admit even to myself the truth about how I was feeling. That afternoon with you when I… I've never taken that risk with anyone, Kassie. Not even all those years ago, when I was an arrogant, dumb youth, determined to score every woman he could—high on exhilaration and the power I had. I never once went without protection. But with you? I lost all control of myself, and that scared me. And then the thought of you pregnant with my child… It wasn't terrifying—it was thrilling. Which in turn was appalling. Was I suddenly some Neanderthal beast who wanted nothing more than to impregnate you and keep you locked in my cave for ever? *So* manipulative. And I denied the truth of that subconscious action and pushed you away.'

He drew in a ragged breath.

'I need to *earn* the right to have you by my side. Become the man you to *want* to be with.'

'You wanted me so badly you didn't bother to stop and think. I was exactly the same. I felt it too. And I wanted it. I was every bit as complicit.'

'But you knew pregnancy wouldn't happen. I didn't. And I took the risk anyway. It was the most selfish moment of my life. And the most telling.'

'I was hurt that you didn't even discuss it with

me. You were just going to get your doctor to come and make me take that medicine. I thought you were horrified at the thought of any kind of future with me.'

'I couldn't bear the thought of manipulating you into a situation that you didn't want to be in. Of imprisoning you with me.' He closed his eyes. 'But at the same time I wanted it so much. *Too* much.'

'So you made yourself give it up?' She understood now. 'You really don't think you deserve happiness.'

'Then I realised that in pushing you away I might be hurting you. I was denying you. And in the end I couldn't do it even to myself. I don't want to let you go.' He drew in a breath. 'But you need to know what you'd be signing up for. Mine isn't a normal life. I have to let you choose.'

'How can you think there is *any* choice?' She gazed at him. 'Don't you *get* how much I love you? I'd do anything for you. I'll put up with anything I have to in order to be with you. I'm not afraid of the media or public interest. I don't care what they think or how they judge me. People have judged me all my life—it wasn't them I hid from. I learned to ignore them and carry on regardless. I'll just put my head down and do what I need to do. And what I *need* to do is love you.' Her eyes filled. 'All I want is to be able to love you the only way I know how.'

'And how is that?'

'Totally. Uncontrollably. With every part of me.'

'And I love you back like that and more. *More*, Kassie, you understand? So much more.'

He swept her into his arms and there was nothing between them but love and joy. In between breathless, urgent kisses they stumbled to her little bedroom and the narrow bed. He eyed it cautiously.

'Too small?' she teased.

'Perfect,' he argued. 'You'll have to cling to me.'

He drew her down on top of him, stripping her as he went.

'I like it when you cling to me. When you sigh…' He kissed her again. 'When you can't stop yourself from wanting me.'

'I never could…' she promised. 'From the moment we met.'

'I ache to give you everything,' he muttered, desperately, tenderly grinding into her. 'To love you.'

The completion she felt at that moment was

so profound that more tears spilled even as she smiled at him. Entwined, they knew the magic they made together was too good to be restrained for long…

He cradled her close afterwards, his voice low. 'I came to the hospital this morning because I couldn't wait any longer. I saw you before you saw me and you looked so happy that I left before speaking with you.'

She heard the remnants of his hurt, understood his vulnerability was still real, and her heart warmed at knowing how deeply he felt about her.

'I'd been to see the head of the prosthetics department to get support for participating in that research project.'

'Oh, that's great.' He sat up and looked down into her face. 'Did you get it?'

'Yes—and they're really keen for me to work on other projects with them too. I should have spoken up sooner.'

'It's never too late.' He drew her closer with a happy sigh. 'That's wonderful.' He stroked her arms. 'You'll keep working there after we're married…?'

She smiled. 'I'd like to…'

'Of course. I'm proud of what you do.'

'But sometimes I'd like to travel with you…to do some of the things you do…'

'We'll work it out,' he promised. 'We'll find some kind of balance.'

'Do you suppose that poor pizza delivery guy is still waiting at the door?' She suddenly sat up.

He laughed and stood, grabbing a towel to wrap around his waist. 'I'll go get it.'

'Like *that*?' she shrieked, appalled. 'There might be photographers out there.'

'I'll be sure to show my best side.' He kissed her swiftly, with an arrogant laugh at her expression. 'I'm with you now—now and always—and I don't give a damn *who* knows.'

EPILOGUE

Six months later

'SHE'S BEAUTIFUL.' KASSIE looked down at the tiny baby nestled in her sister-in-law's arms. 'Just so beautiful.'

'She's tiny.' Giorgos leaned over her shoulder and put on his resting frowny face. '*Too* tiny. She looks like she could break easily. How long until she gets bigger?'

'Giorgos…' Kassie smiled and injected a warning tone into her voice.

'My brother is a marshmallow.' Princess Eleni, currently suffused in a maternal glow, wasn't hearing a bad word about anyone.

'Rest easy.' Damon patted his brother-in-law on the shoulder. 'I've got this.'

Giorgos sighed. 'I know…' He looked again at the petite baby and smiled. 'She's adorable.'

Damon and Eleni had decided their baby should be born in Palisades, so they'd returned to the palace for the last few months before she was due. In a couple of days they'd fly to Damon's private island, to spend time alone and bond together, but they'd just had a personal photo taken, to share with the public, with sweet Princess Antonia only a few hours old.

'You have to admit she is tiny,' Giorgos muttered as he walked with Kassie down the corridor towards their own apartments.

'And that scares you?'

'I'm not afraid to admit that she makes me feel vulnerable. I want to take care of her.'

'Hmm…' Kassie walked ahead of him into the suite. 'You might need to get used to that.'

'Get used to what?' Giorgos shut the door with a definite click.

Kassie turned to face him. She knew not to underestimate the blandness of his query. 'Being around tiny little people who take a few years to grow to their full size.'

He walked towards her slowly, his eyes intent on her. 'What are you telling me?'

'You're a smart man—you *know* what I'm telling you.' She backed up against the wall.

His eyes flickered. *Dangerous.*

'I thought you wanted to wait a while,' he said

in a soft voice. 'We've only been married three months.'

Three months since that insanely massive wedding, with most of the world watching.

While they had created their own traditions, there were some things Giorgos had wanted to do in keeping with his position. Not because it was what had *always* been done, but because he'd wanted the world to know how proud he was to take her as his wife. That had meant an enormous state ceremony, with all the trimmings.

Eleni and Damon had supported her in those terrifying few minutes before she'd had to walk into the country's cathedral, packed with aristocracy, people and news cameras, and not trip her way up that endless aisle with everyone watching.

But she'd locked eyes with Giorgos and her nerves had evaporated. He'd grinned at her, and the whisper of a wink had been a giveaway flash of roguishness. And then his eyes had filled with pure emotion.

The video of that moment had gone viral—made into romantic memes shared millions of times. Suddenly the world had realised that the supposedly 'serious' King not only had a sense of humour, he had a soul, and their love story endlessly dominated the global media.

Fortunately they'd been able to escape to the Summer House for a blissfully private honeymoon.

'And I thought you were on board with that.' She chuckled happily. 'But, no, you've just had to go ahead and be dictatorial and bossy and decide everything for everyone, like the arrogant autocrat that you are.'

'It takes two to tango,' he noted. 'So it can't all be *my* fault.'

'No.' She nodded in agreement. 'And apparently two can become three.'

He inhaled deeply. 'Are you telling me you're pregnant?' His words were little above a whisper.

'Are you telling me you're finally listening?' she teased back breathily.

'Are you telling me you don't think I've already noticed?'

'Oh, *please*.' She paused, frowning as his smug look grew. 'Are you telling me you knew already?'

'Your breasts are fuller...you've been a little more tired than usual. And your period is late.'

He was *that* observant?

She pouted. 'You think you know everything about me.'

'No. I think I don't know you nearly well enough. I can't wait to watch you become a mother. I can't wait to watch you do everything.' He shivered. 'It's been hell, holding off on summoning the doctor to check you over.'

'The doctor already has checked me over,' she reassured him. 'I knew you'd instantly worry, but you don't need to. I'm in perfect health.' She leaned towards him provocatively. 'Apparently I'm in top physical condition.'

'I knew that too,' he growled. 'You tease me too much.'

'You love me for it.' She batted her lashes.

'You do it because *you* love the way I retaliate.' He suddenly reached for her.

'And look where *that's* got me.' She yelped as he pulled her close. 'Happy,' she assured him, meeting the hunger in his kiss. 'So unbelievably happy. And terrified. And excited. I can't believe it!' She laughed with pure, unadulterated delight.

But his smile had gone as tension and intention gripped his muscles. 'I need you. Right now.'

'Yes.' She wound her arms around his neck,

eager to offer the security she knew he sought—of knowing that she was strong and well and happy.

He tugged up her red skirt, knowing just how to draw that desperate response from her. 'Need to feel you,' he groaned as he drove home. 'I'm weak over you.'

She shook her head. Weak was the last thing this man was.

'I never knew I could be this happy.' She cupped his face as she met him, their passion coalescing. 'This fulfilled.'

Their connection blew her away—so constant, so complete.

'Me neither,' he confessed. 'I love you.'

And he didn't just tell her—he showed her. Over and over again. And in the end Kassie couldn't smile for kissing her King, her lover, her *everything*.

* * * * *